It Won't Stay Light Forever

Collected Stories

Also by Ed Weyhing
Speaking from the Heart

It Won't Stay Light Forever

Collected Stories

Ed Weyhing

Fathom Publishing Company

Library of Congress Control Number: 2017944340

ISBN 978-1-888215-25-0 (Paperback)
Ebook ISBN 978-1-888215-26-7 (Kindle edition)
Ebook ISBN 978-1-888215-27-4 (ePub edition)

Publication history of individual stories in this collection:

"The Hundred-Dollar Tip" in *Cimarron Review,* January 1994 (under the title "Sea Gulls"), and in *Generation to Generation,* Papier-Mache Press, 1998.

"Finish Man" in *Short Story,* Spring 1996.

"Condolences" in *Calliope,* Volume 15, Number 1, Fall/Winter 1991.

"Boy in the Wall" in *The Panhandler,* Number 32, 1996 and Abiko Quarterly (Japan), Fall/Winter 1996.

"Honest Work" in *How the Weather Was,* Ampersand Press, 1990, and *Nedge,* 1994, and *Nexus,* 1995.

"How Do You Know?" in *Glimmer Train,* Issue 4, August 1992.

"Harris Steps to the Line" in *Weber Studies,* Winter 1994.

"Empty Gesture" in *Glimmer Train,* Issue 8, August 1993.

"The Walk Will Do Them Good" in *Witness,* Special Issue, American Humor, Volume VII, No. 2, 1993.

"Tales of Destruction" in *Crescent Review,* Fall 1992.

"The Blessing" in *The Providence Sunday Journal Magazine,* August 1987 (under the title "Mister Holmes").

"Turnaround Time" in *Calliope,* Volume 16, Number 1, Fall/Winter 1992.

www.edweyhing.com

www.fathompubishing.com
Fathom Publishing Company
P.O. Box 200448 | Anchorage, Alaska 99520-0448
Telephone /Fax 907-272-3305
Printed in the United States of America

For Stephen, Paul, and Philip

For Mary

Table of Contents

Acknowledgments

Ed himself would have wanted to thank many people who had a part in how he wrote his stories — teachers and fellow students, writing group colleagues, friends and relatives who made comments. Some I am aware of, but many I am not. I have not listed any names for fear of unwittingly leaving someone out. To everyone who helped Ed bring these stories to life, my heartfelt thanks in his name.

For me to say I have deep gratitude to Connie Taylor of Fathom Publishing Company is a pale understatement. Her expertise in publishing, her interest in this story collection, and her unfailing kindness and good humor made all the difference.

Mary Weyhing
August 2017

Introduction

I am delighted to be able to publish this collection of short stories by my late husband Ed Weyhing. He loved short stories, reading them and writing them. He had a great voice and he often read stories aloud to me while I was cooking our meals.

During the spring of 2016, Ed had been gathering his stories, making a few edits, and planning to publish them in a collection. He happened to read each of the stories aloud in the weeks before he unexpectedly died from a stroke.

I am especially happy that Ed had the opportunity to get his stories into the final form he wanted before he died. I feel deep pride in the quality of his writing and in the insight, irony, humor, and compassion he shows in the treatment of his characters. Those were qualities Ed had in everyday life for which he was much loved by people who knew him. Not least by me.

Mary Weyhing
August 2017

The Hundred-Dollar Tip

I figured the old guy was loaded. He lived in one of these houses doesn't look like much till you check out all the wings and additions and sun porches — out each side, the back, and so on — then you realize you're looking at three, three and a half million easy. House I grew up in would have fit in the living room of this guy's house.

He was B. R. Winston, some kind of big shot businessman. Real estate? Wall Street? Junk bonds? Who knows? He was always on the society pages since he retired to Newport a few years back. My job was driving him around once a week.

Mostly I drive a cab. But best of all I like the weeklies. You get to know the people. I drive little old ladies on their errands, haul rich kids to Providence for their ballet. Conversations carry over from week to week. The little old lady tells you her life — her kids, pictures of her grandchildren. And I do great with kids. Never had a sister, just a little brother. But I'm good with the girls, too. Teasing them, of course. Keeping them in stitches. Relationships. It's the best part of my job.

This latest weekly was different. I figured the old guy knew something, maybe had some stories. Maybe some ideas about how I should start my limo business.

As soon as I was introduced to him I gave that up. First off he couldn't even shake hands; he barely put up his left hand. It was a stroke, and besides being paralyzed on his right side he basically couldn't talk — not so I could understand, anyway. For me it was a letdown. How can you get friendly with somebody who can't talk?

But I didn't let that set me back. "All right if I call you Lefty?" I asked. I couldn't tell if he got the joke. Instead, I got this blank look. No sense of humor, nothing.

Also, there was Millicent, the lady who took care of him. Her I couldn't figure out. She looked in good shape for a middle-aged woman. Good figure. A sharp dresser: designer slacks, expensive silk blouses, suits you wouldn't believe. Always looked as if she'd stepped in off Fifth Avenue. Except for her age, you'd never guess she dyed her hair. My mother stopped dyeing her hair after my little brother died. But back when she dyed it — you could tell, believe me.

This Millicent was too young to be his sister. Maybe his daughter, or his niece? His secretary? A nurse? For that matter, she could have been a young wife, relatively speaking. He may have even told me, but I was lucky to catch every tenth word he said. I had nothing against her personally, it was just her attitude. She always referred to him as "Mister Winston," as if I wasn't showing enough respect. But I said to myself, Louie, don't let it bother you. What does it matter, two hours a week? Hey, I'm a professional. My attitude was: do your job, get your money. I still called him Lefty.

She seemed to take good care of him. He was in his eighties, didn't seem very strong, but she always had him shined up top to toe, dressed in these expensive running shoes, some sort of matching exercise suit. Usually she was ready to go out somewhere while I drove him around.

Even though the old guy couldn't talk, the job was okay. Face it: I like to drive. After all, it's my life. Even days off, I'm in my pickup, driving somewhere. I've driven all over — Maine, New Hampshire. During slow times, I take a few days off, drive down to Atlantic City, take in a show or two, drop a little change at the tables.

In this case I drove the old guy's car, a new Buick, loaded with extras. Leather upholstery. It felt like sitting in a lawyer's office. A computerized voice told you everything: The trunk is unlocked. Or: Fasten your seat belt. And power? You should have felt it take the upgrade on the Newport Bridge. When you hit the top, you expected it to keep climbing, right over Jamestown.

Anyway, she laid it out for me the first day. "He enjoys riding around," she said, "seeing things."

"That's what I'm here for," I told her. Fine, lady, I thought. He enjoys riding, we'll ride. He enjoys seeing things, we'll see things.

I got him in and out of the car, no problem. I already knew how to stand a guy up out of a wheelchair, steady him into the front seat. Believe me, I've got some experience doing this. You wouldn't believe how many invalids I've hauled. After I folded his wheelchair and stashed it in the back she handed me a brown tweed golf hat. "In case you get out of the car anywhere," she said.

I took the hat, but thought to myself, Good Luck, Sister! She thinks I'm going to get the old guy out? She's dreaming! You can believe I didn't want any of that responsibility. Maybe I drop him? Then he sues me, gets my license away from me? That's all I need!

That first day I took him over to the mall. There's this drive-up Foto Stop. Girl named Wanda works there. You hand her your cellphone and two minutes later she gives it back with 12 copies of any picture you want on a greeting card. Last year I sent out 12 Christmas cards with me as Santa Claus. I swing through there in my cab sometimes, sit and talk to her till I get a call. If somebody comes up behind me, I just circle around the mall till they're finished.

I thought: He likes to drive, we drove to the mall. He likes to see things, he can see what a beauty this Wanda is. I wondered if that had any effect on him, if he even noticed, you know, girls and all. Anyway, it was pretty obvious the old guy couldn't talk, wouldn't be telling anybody where we went, what we did or didn't do.

The next week was sunny, the Wednesday before Labor Day, and I knew there'd be girls down at Easton's Beach. I drove the old guy down there, pulled right into the parking lot, into the handicapped space. Swear to God, every college girl in New England was down there. We just sat there, took it all in.

Surprised the hell out of me when the old guy said something. "Sea gull," he said. Did he say it? Or did he just make a noise? I don't know. But he leaned forward against the seat belt, pointed up and out the windshield of the car with his left hand — no question what he meant.

There was a good breeze blowing. Up above sea gulls just hung there in the air stream, white wings out, not moving a muscle. Funny how you go somewhere, you see something, but don't really notice it? I suppose I'd forgotten how the sea gulls hung up there so still. And *big!* These were some big birds, hovering right above us, big white wings spread out. Every now and then they moved a feather or two and changed positions. Other than that they just hung up there, sitting on that breeze like they were waiting for something. Waiting for summer to be over? Who knows?

The old guy seemed to like it, sat there in the front seat not saying a word, just looking up at them, out at the waves. I think he liked the whole beach scene — the breeze, the sea gulls, the girls.

With his money, he probably had any girl he wanted, during his time. I wondered what it was like the first time you saw a really good-looking woman, realized it didn't have any effect on you? Of course I didn't say anything to him about it.

When I started the car to leave, the sea gulls broke formation, swooped this way and that, some diving straight at the car. The old guy got agitated, and I had to calm him down. "Hey! It's okay!" I told him. But believe me, I was spooked too.

Next time out was the Wednesday after Labor Day. We went back to the beach. The start of school wiped out the crowds, plus it suddenly cooled off. Even though it was a good day, only a few cars were scattered around the lot. The only people in the water were a couple of surfers in wet suits. There was a good surf, a pretty stiff off-shore wind.

The sea gulls were hanging up there again. They assume every car driving into the parking lot is eating junk food, and ninety percent of the time they're right. They eat a certain amount of shellfish, but they prefer food people leave. Which would *you* rather have, half a double cheeseburger or a couple of raw clams, full of sand? After Labor Day, when the people thin out, the food gets more scarce, and the sea gulls get a little desperate. Any scrap of food and there are plenty of takers, dozens of them swooping down at once.

We pulled up to the beach, and the old guy started saying something. It caught me by surprise, he was so quiet the first two times we went out. I couldn't understand a word of it. I thought it might be about the sea gulls. "Look at those suckers hanging up there, Lefty," I said, but that wasn't it. He kept talking, if you can call it that. It was more like noises than words. Sometimes sort of a moan, but not like pain, more like he was getting my attention.

For all I knew, he had to go to the bathroom, was about to have a seizure, whatever! I tried to say something to calm him down. "Good waves out there today, Lefty!" I said. I didn't know if he understood it or not, or what he understood, or if he understood anything. Still he kept up his talking. I started hearing some of the sounds repeated, though what they meant is anybody's guess. *Rrrrhhhhennigg,* he'd say. *Drremminn.*

That day there weren't more than a dozen people on the beach, mostly mothers with little kids. Almost straight ahead of us a guy was trying to get going on a sail board, but every five yards he flopped over. I joked about it, but the old guy wasn't interested. Instead he just got louder.

I looked around the beach, wondering what to tell him, wondering what to do next. Meanwhile the old guy started moving a little in his seat. His right hand was paralyzed, but he crossed his left hand over and put it on the door handle. Then I knew.

"Hold on, Lefty!" I said. "No way!" I tried to explain we couldn't get out. "In that wind?" I said. "You see that sand blowing sideways?" He was quiet for a few seconds. "Some other day," I told him. "Some day when the weather calms down, we'll give it a shot." I figured that might not be till next summer, which was fine with me.

He seemed a little exhausted. I'm not sure if he resigned himself, or just ran out of gas. Anyway, that shut him up for the day. I would have liked to help, but you've got to draw a line. This time a dozen sea gulls swooped around us as we headed out of the parking lot.

When we came back Millicent talked friendly. "Did you gentlemen have a good ride today?" Believe me, I never volunteered anything. I thought, she's so interested, let the old guy tell her.

The next Wednesday it was raining when I picked him up. He seemed pretty frail, seemed to have gotten weaker. I was a little surprised she sent the old guy out in that weather. With the rain, I knew there'd be nobody at the beach. I took him to Jamestown, out by Beavertail Light. You go right out to the rocky tip of Beavertail Point, then around the lighthouse and back. Rain and spray blew in. Even with the rain, a squadron of sea gulls covered the sky around the lighthouse. You heard them screeching even over the sound of the fog horn, which went off every minute or so. Twenty-five yards out a bell buoy dinged away in the rough seas.

As we swung around the lighthouse, the old guy pointed down at the rocks thirty feet below us, slick and shiny with rain. Waves crashed in, spray flying all the way up to the windshield of the car. Crouched all over the rocks were dozens more sea gulls, looking straight ahead, the weather all around them. Swear to god, some were the size of turkeys, sitting there in the rain, blinking their eyes. I wondered what *their* wing spans would be if they decided to take off. Little did I know.

I told the old guy, as a cab driver I loved rain. Let it rain a few drops, and everybody wanted a cab. "Increased revenue," I told him, in Wall Street terms. He had a few things to say about that. Nothing I understood, of course, but you could tell I got his interest. Hey, I don't mind talking Wall Street, or whatever. I've driven around some high rollers, believe me.

Coming back from Jamestown, we had a half-hour left, so I got us each a Coney Island hot dog at Reba's on Spring Street. Believe me, as low as he looked, the old guy didn't need instructions on how to eat it — one-handed, too. Chomp! Chomp! I figured Coney Islands must be his favorite food. At least he went the whole time without agitating to get out of the car.

But next week he started again. By now it was getting into October, sunny but nippy, no bathing suits at the beach. There was a good wind blowing, and sea gulls hung up there, waiting, facing into the wind. If a car even pulled into the lot, several would peel off, circle around. Anybody got out of a car, there would be dozens. In between, they hung up in the wind, waiting. Sometimes the sky down by the beach was solid sea gulls.

The minute we parked the old guy started up. It was like he wanted to talk, but when he couldn't force the words out, he just got louder. His left hand went over on the door handle. I wondered where he got the energy. You thought he wasn't going to make it from one week to the next, then he'd be full of piss and vinegar, agitating like that.

"Hold on, Lefty!" I said. I tried to think how I could reason with him. I told him I was responsible, asked him what happened if he fell. "I can't lift you," I told him. I said I probably hadn't mentioned my back, the bad disc? "The bottom line is my back," I told him. When my back was okay, I said, I'd get him out of the car, spin him all over the parking lot. "Maybe in a few weeks," I told him. It's amazing what people expect for their money, I thought. I was hired basically as a chauffeur, yet I was supposed to do miracles with the old guy.

I wondered when was the last time he went to the beach. Sometime with his wife? Maybe with his kids, too? Did he even have kids? Believe me, I was sympathetic, but I wasn't about to have a lawsuit, lose my license. Would that have made any sense? Little did I know!

He more or less calmed down after that. Without actually saying it, we came to an understanding. As long as he didn't raise hell at the beach, we could stop for a Coney Island hot dog. He loved the hot dogs, so he pretty much went along with that.

I even came to an understanding with Millicent. She trusted me, and if she had to leave a few minutes early she'd hang the keys to the car on the coat rack, have the old guy dressed and ready in his wheelchair, leave him in the front hall. The cook was always there in the kitchen if the old guy needed her, or if I was delayed. The old guy seemed to like the independence, sitting there waiting for me.

Truth is, though, he seemed to be running out of steam, practically wasting away. I don't think he weighed 110 pounds. Getting him in and out of the car, it was me did all the work. I wondered how much longer he'd be able to go out at all. Did he ever think of that? Did he realize?

At the beach I started rolling down the window on his side. He turned and closed his eyes, faced out the window.

It reminded me of my little brother, the time we went to the beach. He was only about two. We lived in East Providence, and my uncle came down from Worcester to see us. He wanted to go to the beach. It was a weekend in July, and of course there was traffic all the way down, and all the way back, and my father complained the entire trip. That man did not like to drive. Hey, I drive more in a week than that man drove his whole lifetime. Anyway, at the beach, my little brother just closed his eyes and faced straight into the wind. "He's like those sea gulls," my uncle said. We all laughed.

I told the old guy about it: about living in East Providence, growing up there, about that trip to the beach. The old guy listened. Sometimes he looked straight ahead, sometimes he turned and looked out the window. Who knows what he understood, or if he understood anything? Me, I just talked. Hey, I drive a cab. People expect you to talk. Mainly, of course, I talked to keep the old guy calmed down. Let's face it, anything to keep his mind off the fact he couldn't drive his own car, couldn't take a leak without help.

Sometimes I talked to him about driving a cab, told him about fares I had. He would try to say something back. Of course I didn't understand the words, but — it's funny — I started to get the gist of what he was saying, at least whether he liked something, or didn't, whether or not he was impressed.

I told him about the New York fare. It happened one Tuesday night. I picked up my cab just after dinner, to drive the six to six. I went almost to midnight with nothing but nickel and dime fares. I knew it would be even worse from midnight to six. I was glad to have the old guy the next day, so the week wouldn't be a *complete* financial disaster.

Then, *boom!* The dispatcher called any cab in the area. A guy at the Marriott was in a hurry to go to New York City. I was just passing the tattoo parlor on Marlboro Street, so I grabbed the call. I made a U-turn, pulled up in front of the Marriott in eighteen seconds. The guy had his brief case and a cell phone. I got a flat rate from the dispatcher: three-hundred fifteen dollars, including turnpike and bridge tolls. The guy didn't blink an eye, just said, "Let's go." He wanted to know how quick I could get him there. I told him to fasten his seat belt and hang on.

He talked on his phone the entire time, something about a construction job in Manhattan. Believe me: *big bucks.* We flew about two feet off the ground after we got on Ninety-Five, barely slowed down for the toll booths, hit the Triborough Bridge at one minute before three, were at the hotel by twelve minutes after. You should have seen those New York cabbies in front of the Sheraton Midtown wake up when Colonial Cab from Newport went to the front of the line and let the guy out. He pulled out a roll and peeled off three hundreds, a ten and a five, for the fare. Then he peeled off an extra hundred for me. A hundred-dollar tip!

Coming back I took my time, didn't get back to Newport till 8:30 a.m. As soon as I turned my cab in, I went down to Fred's Lunch on Broadway and ordered the #12 breakfast: sausage, eggs, pancakes, the works. By that time the regulars were already in and out. A couple of housewives were having a Danish at the end of their morning walk. I tried to tell Fred about the fare to New York, got his usual enthusiastic reaction. "Regular or decaf?" he wanted to know. Frigging Fred! You sometimes want to wave your hand in front of Fred's eyes, check if anyone's home.

I couldn't wait till that afternoon to tell the old guy. You could see he loved the story, especially the part about driving up in front of the Sheraton. You could tell he appreciated a guy going out and hustling for the extra dollar. You knew he'd done it in his time. It was like he said, *you're on the right track, Louie! You got the right idea!*

The next few Wednesdays we were getting into serious winter, but the old guy still kept going out every week. A few times I worried. How does he make it? How much longer *can* he make it?

Believe me, we talked about everything. I should say *I* talked. About the little old ladies, the rich kids. I told him about driving Angelica Huston to the airport, about taking Jackie Kennedy's sister to the antique stores, about sneaking Robert Redford in sunglasses through the Burger King drive up. I told him my strategy with Wanda at the Foto Stop. I ran the limo idea past him. I could tell he liked it. I knew what he was thinking, what he was trying to tell me. *Go for it, Louie!* he said. *Anything is possible!*

The last day I drove him there were a couple of extra cars in their driveway, one with Connecticut plates. On top of that the old guy was waiting for me outside, in the driveway. I was surprised Millicent left him there, because it was nippy. She had clipped gas money to his sleeve. First I thought it was the usual twenty, then realized it was a hundred. This was strange, too. With all their money, Millicent was careful, never flashed it around.

I tried to sort this out as we drove down to the beach. I was surprised how alert he was, energetic almost, ready to go. I even thought, Hey, maybe he's better. Pretty soon we were just driving along, talking, business as usual. I got to talking some more about growing up in East Providence, about high school, about my old man.

It was cloudy and windy at the beach. The old guy and I had it to ourselves, us and the sea gulls. They were all over the place, even worse than usual. If possible, they seemed even *bigger* than usual. It looked like the ones from Beavertail Light had come over, like they'd come down from Maine, up from Connecticut. There must have been a colony of mussels washed up, and the sea gulls swarmed all over the surf line whenever a wave receded.

I told the old guy about my little brother. He was 10 when I was in high school. He always rode my bike without asking. We fought about it. He had only this dinky hand-me-down two-wheeler from one of our cousins. One day, flying out of our driveway on my bike, he got hit by a car. I came home from high school that day, saw my bike lying on its side on the front lawn. I was pissed, wanted to kill him. "Tony!" I hollered, walking into our yard. Then I saw the bike was bent up, saw people in the house, realized something happened. I felt awful, like I caused it. Telling it to the old guy, I guess I got emotional. I'd never told anyone.

When I finished, the old guy was quiet. For the first time I could remember, he turned and looked right at me, tried to say something. I could see he understood.

Maybe that explains why I got him out. He didn't give me his noise, didn't try to put his hand on the door handle. But I thought, what the hell. "We'll get out," I told him, "but I'll still get you the hot dog." I got his wheelchair out of the trunk, folded it down for him. Some of the sea gulls saw this, started ganging up overhead.

When I got the old guy into his chair, the sea gulls got worse. Some of them swooped down around us. The wind was biting, and when I started to push the chair the sea gulls went really crazy overhead. I was sorry I got him out, but the old guy didn't seem to mind. In fact, he looked up, tried to raise his hand toward them, even said a couple of things, like the first day we saw them. I think he enjoyed it.

Of course that's all they needed, a little encouragement. Dozens more came in out of nowhere. Hundreds of sea gulls, it seemed. Big ones, too, bigger than I'd ever seen, ever imagined. When they got too close I tried to wave them away, but it was like I wasn't even there. They closed right in on us, screeching, flapping their wings all around us, especially around the old guy.

I tried to scare them off, but there was no doing it. Before I knew it, they had hold of the old guy, lifted him right up out of the chair. Funny thing, he didn't seem to mind. He didn't say anything, didn't make his noises, didn't try to break away. He just hung there, closed his eyes, looked into the wind, let himself be carried off like that. When they got him up in the air, they all clustered around, flew away with him. Soon all you could see was a cloud of sea gulls flying away. And just like that, the old guy was gone, without a peep.

My first reaction was, how did it happen? How did he do it? Then I saw his wheelchair, turned on its side and collapsed, where he had left it. And me standing there watching the whole thing like it was an air show. Can you blame me? It was something! I wanted to cheer, like a hockey game.

But I was scared, too. What would I do? Call the police? The Rescue Wagon? And tell them what? The police would never believe this story. There still wasn't another soul at the beach, and by then only a few puny sea gulls scouring the surf line for mussels. I finally decided to take his car back. Maybe think of something along the way? I folded the chair up, put it in the trunk. Believe me, I drove twenty-five all the way back, so there was no chance of getting stopped. It was only 3:15, another forty-five minutes till Millicent was supposed to be home.

But when I got to their house, cars were parked all around the circular driveway. I had to park over to the side, by my pickup. Should I just ring the doorbell? Then what? For a minute I even thought of getting the hell out of there.

A man in a business suit answered the door, but Millicent was right behind him. "Oh, it's Louis." she said. She introduced the guy as Mr. Winston's nephew. You could tell she'd been crying. There were people off in the sitting room, talking quietly. "We tried to call you," Millicent said. Then she broke down, motioned me inside.

The nephew took over, said Mister Winston had passed away during the night. "It was a shock to everyone," he said, "even though Uncle Bart had been failing." He offered to get me a drink.

Needless to say, I wasn't anxious to stay around there. "I'm sorry," I said. "I'm sorry about Mister Winston."

Millicent cried some more and hugged me, tried to get the nephew to pay me for the week, but of course I wouldn't take anything.

It wasn't till I got home I realized I still had the keys to the old guy's car, not to mention the hundred-dollar bill. For a while I worried about how to return them, that is, without a lot of questions and so on. Finally I just put them in the drawer with my socks.

I see them there every day. I think about what the old guy told me, advice about my limo business, about life. I think about what happened.

Believe me, the hundred I'll never spend. But sometimes I wonder what would happen if one day I took those keys, went over there, took the old guy's car for one last drive. Took that sucker to the top of the Newport Bridge. And just took off. Over Jamestown, over Narragansett, over New London, over the Triborough Bridge. Right into the center of New York City before I even touched down, right there in front of the Sheraton Midtown, at the head of the line.

Pressing Hard Enough

Thursday is one of Gabriela's regular cleaning days, but this morning the lady canceled, and Gabriela ended up on the Red Line with nowhere to go, so she rode on out to the Washington Street station to look at the tile. She made the tile in fourth grade: eighteen, nineteen years ago now. All over the city kids made the tiles to decorate pillars in the subway.

Her full name is Gabriela Cardoza, but when they fired her tile it came out GABRIELA CARXXXX. You couldn't read the last four letters of her name. Maybe there was something wrong with the clay. Or the way they fired it. Or maybe she pressed too hard. Her grandmother would have said, "Gabriela, you do everything too hard for a girl."

Or maybe she didn't press hard enough. She didn't know. One of the toughest things to know is the difference between pressing too hard and not pressing hard enough.

They made the tiles with a lady who came in Thursdays after lunch. The Tile Lady had all the tools, and let the students use them. The serrated knife. The convex roller. The awl, which was actually just an ice pick.

Making the tiles was like Art, but the Tile Lady wasn't the regular Art teacher. She just did the tile project.

Some of the kids came out perfect. MAUREEN BISHOP. Every letter just right. Hard enough. Not too hard. Spaced in a nice straight line like the Tile Lady herself did it.

The Tile Lady didn't do a tile, but she showed them the right tools, how to hold them, what they could do. She made suggestions. And she was the only one allowed to use the kiln. She taught the students things about the kiln. How long to do each piece. Why it was so important to get everything right before you fired it. How the clay tile and the glaze actually melt together in the fire.

Gabriela didn't use the roller. Mostly she liked doing it with her hands. Rolling it in a ball between her hands. Flattening it out. The clay — it was grey to start with, but it fired into a dark pink lipstick color. That was the glaze, which you put on before it was fired the last time. Even though you'd think the heat would burn the finish.

She liked doing the tile. Back then she liked school. She was plenty smart enough. Good in math. She even planned to take business math in high school. But when her grandmother got sick, everything started to go downhill. Her grandmother was sick a lot. Then Gabriela started missing. And got behind. When her grandmother died she just quit. She needed to start working anyway.

After her tile was fired once the Tile Lady said it looked nice. "Very nice," she said. "Of course you have to put on the glaze and fire it again." The picture on the tile was okay, but even then you could see some of the letters had baked out flat, so her last name looked like CARXXXX. She asked the Tile Lady about the letters.

The Tile Lady said it was too late to change them. "What's there is there, Gabriela," she said. "Once it's fired that's it." She said people would like her picture, that they wouldn't notice the letters.

Well, *Gabriela* noticed the letters. It was like she hadn't made the tile. Even though the picture came out nice, it was like the tile wasn't really hers.

Sure, the picture was fine. First off it showed her house. Not the place where she lived, but *her* house, the house she built, in her mind. That house had a nice kitchen, like the ladies she works for now, and nice plumbing that worked. And there was no noise. In her mind she still goes and lives there sometimes.

Also the picture had clouds. Gabriela always thought clouds were important. They cooled things down. Maybe caused a little breeze. Even if it meant rain.

And birds. The Tile Lady taught them to do birds by making a V in the clay. For that you used a screwdriver, which the Tile Lady called a blunt tip. You just made a V in the clay. Bump, bump, and you had a bird. Bump, bump, maybe smaller, and you had another bird, farther away.

The Tile Lady told them they could do any design they wanted. Except for their names. For their names, they were supposed to use only letters out of the letter box. The letter box had like steel rods with the letters on the tips, backward. But when you pressed them into the clay the letters came out right. If you pressed hard enough. And not too hard.

Anyway. The house. Clouds. Birds. What we haven't mentioned is the people on the tile. Three in all. Gabriela, and her two children. Gabriela always wanted two children. A boy and a girl. The girl would be a doctor. Actually, back then Gabriela said *an astronaut* or a doctor. She had it all figured out. The girl would be an astronaut or a doctor, the boy would be a president. Not especially the United States. Maybe president of General Motors, or IBM. Some place like that.

And Gabriela, what would she be? Tell the truth, she never really thought what she was supposed to be on the tile. A mother, maybe. The mother of this girl astronaut and boy president.

Anyway, there they were on the tile, the three of them, in front of their house, waiting for the bus. The *bus*, mind you! She didn't think to give them a car. Instead they were waiting for the bus, Gabriela and this future astronaut and future president. And the bus was just coming into sight with the white circle and the big T in the center of it. You made the circle with the cap of a ball point pen. The T is easy to make with the screwdriver.

The two children were harder to draw. She started out making her daughter with the ice pick. That didn't seem right, so she took the tip of her pencil and finished her. Then did her son the president with her pencil, too. She tried to make her daughter a book bag, like she was on her way to school, but at that point things were getting so small. By the time the tile got fired you couldn't tell whether her daughter was carrying a book bag or her lunch, or if it was just a design on her skirt, or what the design was, if anything. Though in Gabriela's mind the book bag had the Space Shuttle and rockets firing off with the astronauts, which is what Gabriela imagined her daughter would be.

So. That was the people on the tile, the three of them. Now you can see them right there in the Washington Street station, third pillar after you come down the steps from the corner right in front of the McDonald's, where the drug store used to be. Gabriela doesn't get out that way often, and when she does she's usually going farther, maybe to a lady in Quincy or someplace. So she would have to get off one train to look at the tile and take a chance the next train would make her late.

But today, after her lady canceled, Gabriela got back on the Red Line, and instead of getting off and changing at Park Street, she just kept going, rode on out there to the Washington Street station. It was the first time she'd got off there since fourth grade. She had wanted to go back and look, go back and see the tile, but she'd never made it before this morning. Maybe she didn't want to see the muddled design on her daughter's book bag. Maybe she didn't want to see the missing letters.

When she got there and saw the tile, it actually wasn't that bad. She just stood and looked at it. And gave herself time to cool down. What we haven't made mention of, what we haven't said is, the lady didn't *call* and cancel ahead of time. She canceled after Gabriela got there. The time before she promised Gabriela forty dollars. Twenty-five regular and fifteen extra for the windows. Forty dollars, they'd agreed on it. But this morning when Gabriela got there the lady was all dressed and ready to leave for work, wanted to give her just thirty dollars. Gabriela reminded her it was forty dollars, like they'd agreed.

"Oh, no, Gabriela," the lady said. "It wasn't that," she said. "It wasn't that at all." Like Gabriela was too stupid to know she was being cheated. And when Gabriela started to tell her again the lady said she didn't have time to argue, and maybe she'd better just cancel for today. And she handed Gabriela three dollars for the subway. It probably took her by surprise when Gabriela didn't give in, didn't even take the three dollars. But just picked up her sweater and her bag and left.

So on the way back Gabriela stayed on the Red Line, just kept right on riding until Washington Street. She got off at Washington Street. Just stood there in the station and looked at the tile and cooled down. She looked at the house and the clouds and the birds until she cooled down, until she couldn't see the muddled design on the book bag, couldn't see the missing letters, couldn't see the CARXXXX anymore. Then she looked at her daughter there on the tile. Holding her book bag. On the other side her son, holding her hand. And there on the tile she saw herself. It's the longest Gabriela ever just stood and looked at anything.

There was a time Gabriela would have given in to the lady, taken the thirty dollars. Or else gotten into an argument she was bound to lose. This time, she figured, what she did was right. Pressing hard enough.

She asked the Tile Lady once, couldn't she change the letters, with a knife or something, so people could read them. "Gabriela," the Tile Lady said. "Gabriela, honey. It's too late for that." She looked Gabriela straight in the eyes, like it was important, something she mustn't forget. "It's simply too late for that," she said. "You've *got* to get everything right while the clay is soft," she said, "before you fire the tile."

Looking at the tile today, this morning, after the lady canceled, Gabriela remembered that. Looking at the tile she thought, we'll see what's too late.

And she closed her eyes and imagined that she invented a way to change the tile even after it was fired. She imagined a whole new tile. She imagined a tile where all the letters were just right. Where the birds, the clouds, the people were right. Where her daughter's book bag looked like a real book bag, with the Space Shuttle and rockets on the side.

Standing there, she felt her son's hand and her daughter's hand in hers. She knew the name on the tile was wrong, that GABRIELA CARXXXX was not her name. My name is Cardoza, she said to herself. My name is Cardoza, Gabriela Cardoza, and my son's name is Philip Cardoza, a journalist and a lawyer and a president of something. And my daughter, she said, my daughter is Alice Maya Cardoza, an astronaut and a doctor. And I am their mother, she said. And I work downtown for an accounting firm. Downtown, in an office.

And for that moment she felt like she actually held the hands of her own children, like she *was* their mother. The mother of a president. The mother of an astronaut, the mother of a doctor.

We'll see what you can still get right, she said to herself.

"Pressing Hard Enough" received Honorable Mention in *Negative Capability's* 1997 Fiction Award.

"Pressing Hard Enough" received Honorable Mention – in the top 25 of 1,000 entrants – in *Glimmer Train's* Very Short Fiction Contest, January 2013.

Empty Gesture

C. K. Barnsworth stretched his neck inside his blue uniform collar, starched up special for Sunday. After church C. K. dropped the wife and kids at home, was just making his rounds before taking home the Sunday paper. Headlines about bribery over in the next county, a highway construction scandal. Not in Tallis County, thought C. K. Not while I'm sheriff. Bottom of the front page was a picture of a school bus in Oklahoma, swept into a stream by flash floods. C. K. thought of his kids on their school buses.

At home C. K. would have Sunday dinner with the family, watch the football game with Albert, his older son. Maybe later he would throw the ball around with C. K. Junior.

C. K. was just about to turn for home when Dispatch called. He reached for the handset to answer.

* * * *

Aron pretended to stretch his arms, letting his right fist reach out the open window. When his hand was just above the roof of the car, where his mom couldn't see, he straightened his middle finger and thrust it forward, goosing the air stream. James Wilson was always flashing the finger. Aron didn't, but he could if the situation called for it. No big deal.

His mom wasn't paying attention. The car slowed down a little as they passed a sign. Food Gas 3 Miles. For breakfast he had eaten some pop tarts they brought from home, and now he was really hungry. He hoped his mom was, too. He pulled his hand back inside. His mom still looked ahead. In the side view mirror he noticed a tow truck with two white guys in it. He wondered how long they'd been back there. They didn't see, he thought. Still, he kept his hands in his lap, his fingers curled into tight fists.

* * * *

Dispatch told C. K. Old Samuels phoned in. Said he heard poachers over in the woods behind Tallis Country Tavern. Old

Samuels was a touchy one. Actually, everybody was a little touchy since the Tavern caught fire two months ago.

Fire almost went out by itself. C. K.'s deputy found it smoldering. Wrecked the kitchen and the ladies rest room. Ruined all the electrical. Pretty well smoked up everything else. Then water damage to boot, and a busted-in door, after they called the volunteers down there to put it out. The volunteers never thought to see if they could get in the back, where the fire was, with less damage. Just busted right in through the front door, leading a hose across tablecloths, knocking salt and peppers everywhere. C. K. noticed the electrical when he got there. Called Whitley Valley Power over to shut it off. Lucky for the volunteers they wasn't all electrocuted. By the time old man Tallis got down there he couldn't even boil water in his own restaurant. Had to stand the volunteers to coffee and doughnuts over at The Breakfast Barn on Two Gates Road.

Everybody had an opinion about the fire. Some said poachers did it. Said they must have been hunting back in the woods, behind the Tavern. Shooting, drinking. Some guessed they hadn't started out to break in, hadn't meant to start a fire, but got juiced up, climbed in through an open window or something. Old Samuels guessed they must have took offense when the refrigerator was locked.

The volunteer chief agreed it was poachers. But then a few of the volunteers said one of the colored might of done it. Colored dishwasher from over to Ring City quit the restaurant the week before. But Old Man Tallis said he had no malice with the colored, nor they with him.

C. K. himself investigated, could find no sign of forced entry. Anyway, turned out the colored dishwasher had been out of there over a week before the fire, took the bus to Chicago.

What C. K. *did* find was the switch box charred out completely. "Circuit Breaker shorted out," he told the insurance fellow, who wrote that on his clipboard. "Electrical fire," C. K. dictated. He showed the insurance fellow how the service line coming in wasn't big enough to support the electric fry grill Old Man Tallis added three years before.

Poachers! he thought. The colored! Too many people with time on their hands, thinking up stories, looking for Tallis County to turn into a TV show. Maybe they should spend their time learning electrical, like C. K. had.

The most edgy was those with time on their hands. All the time calling in, reporting this and that. *Poachers over on Bigelow's farm. Disturbance down to Ring City. Saw two men with guns out by the quarry. One of them colored.* Sure, thought C. K. Always with guns, always one of them colored. If C. K. could put together all the men with guns reported in Tallis County over the last ten years, he would have a fully-armed battalion of phantom riflemen, half colored, half white trash. And a full battalion of busybodies to report on them.

C. K. learned to shoot when he was 10. Had his own gun. Taught both his boys. Bought them *their* first guns. Only let them shoot in season, though, when he was with them. Or at the Fish and Game Club range. Taught them respect for guns, respect for the law. That's the problem. Parents not willing to teach their kids respect: for guns, for anything.

C. K. swung his car around and headed down West Point Road, toward the interstate. Toward the Tallis Country Tavern.

* * * *

Once in school James Wilson flashed the middle finger when Mrs. McNulty was stopped in the aisle looking at Carla Thompson's workbook. It made Aron laugh. In fact all the boys laughed, and Mrs. McNulty turned around and almost caught James Wilson.

Everybody in fifth grade was white except Aron and James and a couple of the girls. James was 12, bigger than the other boys in fifth grade, who were nine or ten. Aron was nine. Like Aron, James was good at football, but sometimes he got in trouble. Aron's mom told him, "Just make sure *you* don't get in trouble." She meant it.

The truck settled in just behind his mom's car. On its bumper was a red, white, and blue rebel flag.

The tow truck stayed right in line behind them. The guys were wearing sunglasses. They nodded their heads in time, like listening to music. Aron could almost hear the music from their radio. Their sunglasses were mirrors, like state troopers'.

His mom's radio had played most of the way from Louisville. Now the only noise was the hum-and-click, hum-and-click of the tires on the freeway.

"Mom, can we turn the radio on?" Aron asked.

"Sugar, it will just be preachers and gospel music. Let's just leave it off and let it be quiet for a while."

It was Sunday morning. At home they usually went to church. Aron got up before his mom, made pop tarts and orange juice. His mom taught him how to make French toast, but she wanted to be there when he worked the stove.

When Emerson, his mom's boyfriend, stayed over, he came out in the morning and congratulated Aron with a high five hand slap, like he'd just scored a touchdown. "My man!" Emerson would say to him. "*Excellent* orange juice, my man!"

Emerson taught him pinball on the machine at KMart. Emerson wouldn't play football, though. When Aron tried to get him to play football, Emerson messed around and acted like his legs were turning to jelly. He wasn't serious about football like Aron.

Last night in the truck stop, his mom let him have one quarter to play pinball. Afterward they slept awhile in the car.

Aron woke once in the dark to see the cab of a big truck growling slowly past the window of the car, just on the other side of the glass. The name on the truck was *Mack*. Fleetwood Mac: that was the music his mom liked, not gospel.

She knew how to dance, and knew the names of all the wild flowers she found on their picnics. If they played catch, she was better than Emerson. Also she could lip sync Whitney Houston. Right now, though, his mom was worried about Gram.

Once Aron caught the flu, and his mom was worried about him. She fixed him tea and mashed potatoes and buttered toast on a tray, because that's all he felt like eating. Then she sat on the side of the bed and showed him the photograph album: pictures of when he was a baby, pictures of his father's graduation, pictures of them taking him to the zoo. But his mom never got sick. "She's a tough woman," his father sometimes said.

Even after they were apart, his father bragged about her. Once, in the barber shop, his father pulled out a snapshot of their wedding. In the picture Aron's mom had only one good eye. The other had been carefully made up beneath the white veil, but it was swollen, only half open.

His father was in the barber chair, Aron waiting. "Two days before the wedding," his father said, "Lucille was teaching her dance class at the Y." He stopped and looked around seriously at everyone. One of the old guys reached up and turned the TV volume down, while the barber kept the scissors moving. "Lucille's been dancing since she was about three," Aron's father said. "Trying to teach some gal to do one of those fancy twirls, gal elbowed her in the eye." His father said she finished up the class, then played league volleyball for an hour and a half before she did anything for the eye. The old guys looked at the picture and laughed.

His mom said her wedding day was the only time in her life she ever had a black eye. "You better not get any black eyes fighting." Sometimes there were fights on the playground, but Aron kept clear. He'd stick to football. The old guys in the barber shop got him to show his muscle, but Aron's father said it's brains that would make him a winner, not his muscle. *"Think,"* his father would tell him. "Try to think what the other guy will do next."

Food Gas Next Exit, the sign said.

"This is the last time to eat until Gram's," his mom said, easing over into the exit. The truck pulled over with them. "Let's don't have a lot of running around. We got to make better time, or we'll *never* get there."

They started from Louisville yesterday, just after Aunt Jo called about Gram. Aron's mom called Emerson at work and told him. Normally he would have come and stayed over last night. Instead he had brought his VW over for them to drive. Then she called Aron's father and told him. He must have asked about keeping Aron.

"No, he should come with me," his mom said on the phone. "I think this may be it."

Gram had been sick before, but they didn't drive to Norfolk every time she was just *sick*. And Aron's mom hadn't been this quiet the other times.

Usually Aron went to his father's apartment on Sunday. They played football behind the complex, ate lunch at The Shrimp Roll, then watched the football game. That Sunday it would have been the Indianapolis Colts vs. the Atlanta Falcons.

Would Uncle Jake have the football game on? Probably not if Gram was really dying.

At the end of the exit ramp was a stop sign. A two-lane road went under the freeway through a heavy stand of pine. Aron saw an *Eat* sign on a post at the edge of the road. Back from the road, three gasoline pumps stood outside a small square restaurant.

The tires made a low gargling sound across the gravel parking lot. Theirs was the only car. Aron's mom drove straight for the front door of the restaurant, but it was closed.

"Well, there must be *some* place down this road to eat," she said.

The tow truck had followed them. It stopped at the edge of the parking lot, to let Aron's mom go first. "They must be looking, too," she said, pulling ahead. "I hope they don't expect *me* to find someplace. It's the blind leading the blind."

Aron could see both the guys. They didn't act like they had seen him flash the finger.

Beyond the restaurant the road entered the trees again, no grass, just a brown blanket of pine needles. The trees grew close to the road, and Aron had to lean out the window and look up to see the bright blue Sunday morning sky they left back on the freeway. It was almost like they were driving inside, down a winding corridor through the pines. Behind them Aron heard the roar of an eighteen wheeler heading down the freeway they just left.

In the mirror he watched the rebel tow truck following them. Occasionally it dropped out of sight around a curve, then reappeared. They didn't see me, Aron thought. He wondered if he should give the peace sign, just in case. His father taught him "V for victory," but Emerson said it was the peace sign.

Playing football, Aron's father didn't mess around. He was serious about football. He played with Aron for hours.

"Down, hut one, hut *two!*" his father called out, just behind him. Aron snapped the ball to him, then ran down field. Faked right, cut left, hooked in, turned around. Just as he turned around, his father fired the ball.

Aron's father taught him the post pattern, and down and out. Aron was good at catching it, too. "First down!" his father called out to him if he made a good catch. "Touchdown!" if it was a really good catch.

Once Aron touched the ball down in the imaginary end zone, then held it high in the air, moving his hips in the start of the dance steps Emerson taught him.

"Nullified because of a penalty!" his father called out. "The wide receiver was offside." Aron knew he wasn't offside: the penalty was for doing the dance steps.

"That jive stuff won't win you no football games, Aron," his father said.

On the playground Aron still celebrated when he made a good catch. But with his father he did not dance with the ball.

Cars passed on the narrow road, going in the other direction: fathers in ties, girls in bright dresses, coming from church. Aron wished he was heading home for dinner.

Around a curve, Aron's mom pulled off the road at another *Eat* sign. Under a CocaCola emblem the sign read: *Tallis Country Tavern, Sandwiches, Salad Bar, Breakfast All Day.* The restaurant sat back from the road. Brick siding covered the walls, just like Gram's house in Norfolk.

Then, at the back of the restaurant, Aron saw the white trim smoked black. The brick siding was charred, partially pulled away from the walls. Two charred chairs were thrown on a dumpster at the side.

Aron's mom crept the car ahead, looking at the damage. "So much for this exit," she said. "Maybe we'll just go back and try the next one."

As she started up again, the tow truck pulled into the parking lot and crunched straight across the gravel, yellow lights blinking. His mom stopped. The truck pulled alongside her window. There was a red star on the door. *Tallis Texaco,* it read. Aron could hear women singing a country song on the radio. Chimes and guitars backed up the singers.

The man in the side seat spoke to Aron's mom. "Looks like this one's closed, too, Sister. Too bad. Wonder how a fire like that ever got started."

The man had a sun tan like a lifeguard's, and a yellow mustache that curled down at the sides, like old time pictures. He wore a baseball hat with a patch that said *John Deere.* Yellow curly hair stuck out from beneath the hat. John Deere leaned out the window of the tow truck with both elbows on the frame, propping his chin in his hands. He looked down at Aron's mom through the sunglasses.

"Too bad it's closed," he repeated. "Me and Thurman was going to buy you lunch, Sister." Thurman had a goatee like Emerson's. He looked at Aron's mom and smiled. Aron saw two hunting rifles on a rack inside the truck.

John Deere looked their car up and down. "We towed one of these little German cars once, Sister. Feels good up on the hook. Gotta watch 'em, though. They fall apart. But anyway, how would you and the youngster like a plate of sausage and eggs?" John Deere said.

"Thank you, but we've already had breakfast," Aron's mom said. "We've got to get going." Aron swallowed hard.

She started to pull ahead and continue out of the lot. Thurman moved the truck ahead and kept right beside her. She couldn't turn back out to the road. She laughed nervously, stopping the car. "Whoa, there, Thurman," said John Deere, holding up a hand. "The lady is trying to drive her car. Can't you see you're in the way?"

Aron's mom pulled ahead again, but Thurman moved ahead and stayed even. A pickup truck rumbled down the road toward the freeway. "Sorry, ma'am," said John Deere out the window, after they both stopped again. "Thurman ain't the best driver in the world, but he tries hard."

Aron wished they were out of there, getting breakfast or lunch somewhere. Aron heard another eighteen wheeler on the freeway, by then in the distance behind them.

Aron's mom had pulled ahead almost to the trees at the edge of the parking lot, and was still not turned back toward the road. She clicked the car into reverse and started to back up. The tow truck backed also, staying alongside.

"Hold it, Thurman, the lady's backing up," said John Deere. He turned to Aron's mom. "Wait, now let's get this organized. Thurman here thought you was going ahead. Which is it, ahead or back?"

"I'm trying to get back out on the road, but there wasn't room to turn..."

John Deere talked over the top of her. "Oh, oh! Not room to turn. Must be a steering problem. That's the thing about these German cars, Sister. But don't worry, we can fix it." He suggested they get something to eat first.

Aron's mom thanked him, and said they weren't hungry. "The car is okay," she said. "We just need to be getting on."

"Not with a steering problem," said John Deere. He got out of the truck. "No way we would let you take the youngster back out on the road with a steering problem." He looked across at Aron, back to his mom. He mentioned a restaurant in a place called West Point. "The boy is probably hungry. You shouldn't be out there driving, you with a steering problem, the boy hungry." His talk got louder and faster.

Aron wondered if the guys had seen him flash the finger, and were getting even. John Deere moved around to the front of the car and unlatched the hood. "I'll check the steering out for you right now," he said. "Then we can go to lunch and you'll be safe to go on your way. *Everybody's* got to eat."

"Please don't fix anything," said Aron's mom. "We'll be okay. Thanks for offering, but we don't need anything. We just need to be getting on."

John Deere didn't answer. "Put the damn hood down and let us go," Aron's mom shouted.

"Hear that, Thurman? All your crazy driving has got Sister upset. Why don't you make it up to her by checking her rear end for her."

Thurman got out of the truck and walked around behind the car. In the side mirror he crouched down beside the rear wheel, and put his hand on the tire. Aron heard a hissing sound.

His mom leaned on the horn. It sounded higher and louder with the hood up. John Deere did something under the hood. The horn fluttered and stopped.

"You got quite a horn there, Sister. Hard to think under there with it going." He appeared from behind the hood, holding up a small piece of wire. "Anyway, one of the wires come loose. It's just one more thing. Just take me and Thurman that much longer, with the steering and all."

"Son of a bitch," Aron's mom said under her breath.

Whoa! Aron thought. He wondered what she thought the guys would do. He knew he was in trouble if she found out he had been flashing the finger.

Thurman stood up from the right rear wheel. "Tire's flat," he said to John Deere. In the side mirror, Aron saw him smile.

"Well, can you imagine that, Thurman? Sister, you were fixin' to take the boy out on the road in *this car,* him hungry, you with a flat tire, your horn broke, on top of a steering problem, too?"

John Deere looked at their license plate. "In Kentucky that may be your idea of safe, but here we protect our children better. You all better come with us and let us get this boy some lunch before you get busted by the police. Now *there* you talkin' real delay. You get busted you may have to make bail. You got bail money with you, Sister?" He was under the hood again. Aron didn't know how much bail cost, or how much his mom had.

"Listen, you guys," his mom said, "this isn't funny anymore. We really have to get going now. We're trying to... I've got a family emergency..."

"Oh, Sister, I could tell it was an emergency, by how fast you' checking out all these road houses. Anyway, it ain't us holding you up," John Deere said, walking around to her side. "I'd like to let you be on your way right now. But you can't go driving out like this: flat tire, steering problems. I've told you, just have lunch with us and we'll fix you up and get you back on the road. We're trying to be accommodating. I think you need to think more about the boy's safety. Anybody can see that boy's hungry. And this car: you wouldn't make it fifteen feet, the condition this car is in."

Aron squeezed the fingers of his right hand together in his lap.

John Deere was looking at a dark plastic object in his hand. "Why don't you try starting it now?" he said to Aron's mom.

She cranked the starter. It ground several seconds. The engine didn't catch. She tried it again. Same thing.

"Just what I thought," said John Deere, holding up the dark plastic part. "It's the rotor. The rotor ain't even in the distributor. You'll never get it started like that. We'll need to fix that, too. Replace the rotor. Fix the steering. Fix your horn. Fix your flat. You be glad Thurman and me know cars," said John Deere. He went on about wanting to help. "We all need help sometime or other," he said.

Then he started in about lunch again, opening the truck door and holding it like a limousine driver, gesturing that Aron and his mom could climb into the cab. "We can all ride together," he said.

A song on the radio was just ending. "... *Sweet Jesus. Amen.*"

"Boy ever ride in a tow truck?" John Deere asked.

"You pervert!" Aron's mom said in a low voice, rolling her window up. She locked her door, reached across and locked Aron's, told him to roll up his window.

"Sister, who *you* calling a pervert? To talk like that in front of that young boy!" John Deere was shouting, to be heard through the closed windows. Behind him, a commercial on the truck radio competed for attention. "*AhhhWOOOOOOO!*" howled a studio goblin.

John Deere rambled on: "What's your case worker say, she hear you talk about perverts in front of the boy?" He hollered about no gratitude, about how he just wanted to help.

"Halloween clearance sale...," the radio said. Something about sedans, pickups, and fourbyes. *"...sticker price!"* Witches cackled in the background.

Then John Deere slammed the truck door, and took a rag out of his pocket and wiped his hands. "Anyway, we seen you giving us the come-on back there, waving the finger out the window and all." Aron felt himself blush, but his mom didn't react. She sat with her arms folded on the steering wheel, staring into the dashboard.

John Deere walked around the front of the car and put the hood down. Aron's mom looked up at him.

"You're lucky, Sister," he said, shaking his finger at her. "You're lucky Thurman and me don't bear no malice. All we been through down here. This fire. Wasn't for this fire, we could've all got us some lunch right here." John Deere motioned toward the charred restaurant. "Know who set that fire, Sister? Wasn't no *enemy* set that fire. My granddaddy don't have no enemies."

John Deere's face was getting red. He was plenty mad about the fire. And not just mad, Aron thought. He looked a little crazy. When he mentioned his grandfather, his voice wavered. He seemed about to cry. He said a boy who worked for his grandfather had set the fire on purpose.

"That's *thanks,*" he said. "All my granddaddy did for him, then pull a trick like that." John Deere reached inside the truck and pulled out one of the hunting rifles. He held it up for Aron's mom to see. Said he had to carry the rifle for protection. "That's the *thanks* you get," he said again, raising the rifle to his shoulder and pointing it at the restaurant.

Aron looked toward the restaurant. John Deere talked while aiming the rifle. "That's..." Crack! "...the thanks you get." Aron jumped when he heard the gun fire, and saw a piece of burnt siding fly off the corner of the building. A flock of starlings rose from the pine trees, heading back across the clearing toward the freeway.

John Deere aimed again. "That's..." *Crack!* "...the thanks you get." A piece of the aluminum downspout, black with smoke, spun up in the air, landing in a patch of grass beside the building. Thurman had walked around the truck, and stood beside John Deere.

"C'mon, Gerald," said Thurman. "Let's get on out of here."

"Hell, no," said John Deere. "We've made a commitment. We been asked to help; that's what we'll do: help." He leaned back toward Aron's mom and gestured, waving the gun toward the land beyond the empty clearing. "Down here we believe in commitment, Sister." Aron couldn't remember what "commitment" meant. He imagined hundreds of people lurking in the nearby woods, believing in commitment.

"Okay, fine," said Thurman, "but then let's put the gun away and get it over with. All this hollerin' and shootin'. You're gonna have C. K. down here. C. K. calls my daddy again, he'll shit."

John Deere returned the gun to the rack in the back of the truck cab, slammed the door, then walked back to the front of the car. He nodded toward Thurman, then glanced under the front bumper. "Okay, let's put her on the hook. See if you can do it without messin' up Sister's fine German car."

A noisy grey junker roared through the clearing. A teenager was driving. As they passed, a girl in the passenger seat looked blankly at the tow truck and the disabled car. Thurman got back in the tow truck and pulled it in front of the car. The yellow lights still blinked silently.

* * * *

C. K. wished he was home, but here he was, driving in the opposite direction. It was sunny, but the heavy stand of pine shaded the road from both sides. The Pine Tunnel, his wife called it. It was like driving inside, inside a fragrant green tunnel, the sun only coming through here and there in a clearing amongst the trees. C. K. slept in these woods, first as a kid himself, then with his own kids. His daddy taught him how to make a bed of pine boughs. He taught his kids.

Their wedding day, they came this road. C. K. Barnsworth and Hallie Ann Jameson: a big wedding back then. Had the reception at the Tallis Country Tavern. Had the whole place to themselves: there was 60 or 70 cars in that parking lot. Aunts and uncles and cousins all the way from Tennessee, some from West Virginia. When him and Hallie was ready to leave, guys in the wedding party tried to box their car in, but C. K. found a path out between the pine trees, driving right through the edge of the woods, bridesmaids all screaming and waving, kids throwing firecrackers after them, Hallie laughing and crying both at once.

Just when he was remembering this, C. K. heard the shot, heard it himself. Not a long ways off. Then another shot. Sounded like down the road toward the interstate, but it was hard to tell. C. K. looked, listened. Hard to tell from here. Could be poachers. Could be nothing.

Down the road it was quiet. Nothing in the trees but the scent of pine. Only a car or two on the road, some still dwindling in from church. Then he heard a rumble, and it turned into the sound of a bad muffler on the road ahead. An old grey Chevy appeared through the trees. Carson Cecil's kid, Billy. Ran around with C. K.'s Albert sometimes. Girl in the seat beside him, half in his lap. When they saw C. K., the girl straightened out in the seat, Billy waved sheepishly, throttling back to 35 or so. The engine coughed and backfired.

Bingo! thought C. K. The poacher was most likely Billy Cecil's junker, backfiring its way around the county. Old Samuels wouldn't know the difference. They'd likely be getting calls about it all day.

* * * *

John Deere unfastened a hook on a chain from the bed of the truck and led it toward the front of the car. The chain rattled over the edge of the truck.

"Now, Sister, we want to do this without messin' up your car. I say a commitment is a commitment. Just put the car in neutral and undo the brakes."

Aron saw his mom move her foot over onto the brake pedal. When the brake light came on, John Deere smacked the palm of his hand on the hood of the car and shouted.

"I'm a little surprised at your moral fiber, Sister," he said. "That you'd not show more commitment in front of the youngster." His face was getting red again, and spit was forming at the edge of his mouth. "I don't know about Kentucky, but over here a commitment means just that: a commitment. *You ask for help, that's a commitment!*"

Thurman had gotten out of the truck again and walked back toward John Deere. "Gerald," he said, raising his hand. "There's no sense gettin' all riled up." He put a hand on John Deere' shoulder.

"You shut up!" John Deere said, brushing him away. He stabbed his finger at Aron's mother. "That's why a boy would burn up my granddaddy's restaurant. *No moral values! No commitment!*"

Aron knew they were in deep trouble. He didn't mean anything by flashing the finger, hadn't even known they were there. Geez!

"This is takin' too long," said Thurman. "All this talk! We're not gettin' anywhere here. She ain't gonna do nothin'. Let's get on outta here."

John Deere stopped and caught his breath. "You shut up and get back in the truck," he told Thurman. "You're forgettin' who got you off the hook with C. K. and your daddy Friday night." He sized up the distance between the truck and the car. "I'll work the hook," he said. "You're gonna have to back a little closer so she don't have to drag so far."

Aron's mom told him under her breath, "Whatever they do, just keep your door locked and the windows up. Broad daylight, they won't break through the windows, and they're not about to shoot anybody. This is just their stupid idea of how to scare us. This is their perverted idea of fun."

Aron buried both fists deep in his lap, between his legs. He thought he could hear another car coming down the road. Thurman got back in the truck and eased it closer. John Deere worked the winch to keep the tow chain taut.

* * * *

Now through the trees C. K. saw flashing yellow lights in the clearing ahead. Red, white, and blue tow truck. Tallis Texaco. Old man Tallis's grandson, Gerald. Him and his sidekick. Had enough of them Friday night: both drunk, leaving the dance, driving their car across the lawn of the VFW after the rain. Six-inch-deep ruts. Well, at least today they're working, for a change. Got themselves a tow. Colored girl, her kid. Foreign car.

C. K. swung into the gravel parking lot. Gerald was just putting her up on the hook, gave him a thumbs up. Colored girl looked scared spitless. She oughta be, C. K. thought. Buying these foreign cars. Use their Master Cards to gas them up. Don't know how to take care of them. Then wonder why they crap out in the middle of nowhere.

Gerald looked like butter wouldn't melt in his mouth. On his best behavior, after Friday night. Better be! thought C. K. Gonna run that kid in one of these days. Even if he *is* Old Man Tallis's grandson. Him and his halfwit friend, smiling away, as usual. Wouldn't hurt the both of them to stay off the booze. Maybe having a tow or two today will keep them out of trouble. And if it don't, C. K. thought, I don't really want to know about it.

* * * *

Even through the trees Aron recognized it as a police car. It slowed down when it came into the clearing. The car was khaki, with a white stripe down the side, red and blue lights on the top. *Tallis County Sheriff* was printed along the white stripe. The car slowed down and turned into the parking lot.

Thurman stepped down out of the truck and said something Aron didn't hear. John Deere told him to shut up, then waved toward the police car and gave a thumbs-up sign. The sun in the clearing reflected off the windshield of the police car. Aron barely saw the man inside wave back. Then the brown car made a U-turn on the gravel and pulled back out to the edge of the road.

"Oh, no!" his mom said. Thurman moved back and leaned against her door. She started rolling down her window. "Officer!" she called out after the police car. *"Officer!"*

Down, hut one, Aron thought to himself. Hut TWO! He snapped the button lock up and opened the car door. "Aron, don't!" his mom called out.

But already he was on the gravel. John Deere dropped the tow chain and ran around the truck, holding both arms out to block him. Then Aron remembered what commitment was. Don't make your cut, his father had told him, until the defender commits himself. Aron faked to the right, and John Deere committed himself. He lunged for Aron. Aron cut back to the left and passed him, hooking down toward the police car. John Deere slipped on the gravel and went down. Post pattern, Aron thought, his sneakers digging in for the dash down field. Behind him there was a laugh, and John Deere swearing.

* * * *

Before pulling back out onto the road, C. K. stopped and looked to his left, down toward the interstate. He *could* check out the remaining three miles to the county line, just so's he could tell old Samuels he had. Hell, thought C. K. There's no poachers down here. No poachers anywhere. Besides, Dispatch was calling, saying Hallie was on the phone, wanting to know when he'd be rolling in for Sunday dinner. "Ten four," said C. K. "I'm just leaving the Tavern, heading right in. Be there in five, ten minutes."

* * * *

When the police car hesitated at the edge of the road, Aron tried to run harder, but his feet slipped in the gravel. Arms flailing, he caught himself and kept running. By then he was directly behind the car. Down and out, he thought, waving his arms at the car and running full out. "Wait!" Aron shouted. He could hear the police radio crackling. The sheriff looked to the left, toward the freeway, then started to turn up the road in the other direction. *"Wait!"* Aron shouted. But the car pulled away, kicking up gravel behind it. Aron kept running toward the road.

* * * *

C. K. didn't usually swear over the air, but when Dispatch said one of the VFW had called to ask why they wasn't displaying the flag, he snapped back. "Well why the hell ain't you?" Dispatch answered that one of the pulleys on the flagpole was busted. C. K. turned right and gunned it out of the parking lot, spraying gravel.

* * * *

Running downfield, Aron passed the first two defenders, pushed aside the third. A purple helmet tried to spear him out of bounds, but he sidestepped, then headed down the sideline, gaining speed, his feet barely touching the ground. Other purple helmets flooded onto the field from the sidelines, even though the play was running. He ran through them, around them, pushed them aside, faced still more. Across the thirty-yard line, the twenty. Purple helmets from the other side of the field veered over to cover him. He knew the ball was in the air. He looked back for it, found it spiraling against the clouds. Purple helmets were all around him, bumping him, trying to stay ahead of him. He saw one of them raise an arm, go up. Too soon, he thought, knowing the trajectory of the ball. Another step, then Aron went up, putting all his strength and stretch into the leap. Hands tried to pull him back to earth. The pass would be long, he thought, and he stretched higher for it. He *thought* himself higher, higher than the purple helmets, higher than the outstretched hands, floating up to intersect the flight of the ball. Then he saw the ball pass into the face of the sun, come out glowing itself, a fireball flaring down out of the sky. He saw the blazing oval touch his fingertips, his hand, his wrist. Still floating, he saw himself gather it against his blue jersey, holding it for the final glide into the end zone, waiting for the signal of the referee, waiting for the impact.

* * * *

i said sugar grab that box of pop tarts and a couple of apples
he washed the apples and put them in a bag like his school lunch
we ate them together that night
> *the moon was out and we drove late*
he was never a minute's trouble in school or in the neighborhood
i was worried when we first moved there
> *but the neighbors all loved him*
> *he played with all the kids*
> *he did fine*
him and emerson and that pinball
maybe emerson was good for him
his daddy was always so serious
after four o'clock i couldn't sleep any more and i wanted to get going
> *so i made sure his seat belt was okay*
and started out again
> *he was so peaceful*
he stayed asleep until it got light
i knew he was just a child
> *but with mama dyin i wanted him along*
> *i thought of the first time my mama held him*
she'd touched his forehead and said it was like my daddy's
i couldn't remember
it seemed like it was taking us so long
i didn't want to take time to stop for breakfast
he ate the last of the pop tarts riding along in the car

* * * *

Thirty yards down the road, C. K. had just reached down to replace the handset when there were two shots. No backfire this time. Sounded like it was right beside his car, right under him, all over the trees behind him.

"Oh God," he said out loud. He didn't want to believe the shots had come from the clearing, the clearing where he had turned around 15 seconds earlier. He didn't want to stop. Didn't want to turn the red and blue lights on, throw the car in reverse. As he reached the clearing, he didn't want to see the two men, wrestling each other against the side of the truck, the rifle on the ground beside them, yellow lights still blinking above their heads. He didn't want to hear the colored girl's scream, didn't want to see her running across the gravel, the tail of her blouse flying loose.

He didn't want it to be her kid, in the blue football jersey, number 88, legs twisted funny, one sneaker missing, five feet away from the road, lying on his back in the gravel, looking straight up in the air.

He grabbed up the handset by reflex. But twice he pushed the button, and the words wouldn't come, only a low moan, rising from somewhere deep inside the starched uniform shirt. After that his voice returned, and he made the call. "Code Double Zero!" he told Dispatch. "I want another car and an ambulance over to the Tavern!" But as he got out of the car and started into the clearing, C. K. knew the ambulance was only an empty gesture.

A Message from Todd

Are other parents like me? You want to hear your kid say how you did as a parent. If you did great, they take it for granted. If not, well, they probably don't want to discuss it.

With Todd, I did my best. I wasn't perfect. At times we didn't do well with each other. You want to be positive, to be encouraging. Yet some things you can't ignore. That's what discipline is all about. But the discipline takes its toll: bad feeling, bitterness. Before you know it you're on different planets.

Now I'd be willing to listen. I'd like to know: What could I have done better? What if I had done such and such? What if I had another chance? I wish I knew what he'd say.

Last time we heard from him was before he went back to the Gulf, over a year ago. He first went over there in 1990 as a Navy diver, an underwater demolition expert. Then when his enlistment expired he went back to Saudi Arabia with Aramco, as a civilian. There's still thousands of unexploded shells, mines, God knows what else, so his services are much in demand. With overseas pay he probably makes twice as much as I do. But he was only back in the states a few weeks, no time for them to come to New England for a visit. Now he has a four-month-old son he hasn't even seen.

I don't mean to complain. There's plenty to be grateful for. His wife, Christina, is the sweetest thing. She keeps us up to date on the grandchildren, Todd Jr., the four-month-old, and Jennifer, who's three. Christina calls, writes, sends pictures. You'd think *she* was our child. They called a couple of times when Todd was back here those few weeks. He came on the line for a few sentences, left most of the talking to Christina. If it weren't for her I wonder if he would have called at all.

I suppose I should stop worrying. What's done is done. But I can't help thinking about it. It's the stress, Todd still over there.

Plus something that happened just after the war ended. A guy called, just discharged from the Navy, said he knew Todd.

I'm the membership chairman for the local VFW, so I get a lot of phone calls from servicemen. Occasionally they'll come to work for us. Perkowski, my partner, was Third Armored Cavalry, like me. When we came home in 1971 we both went to work for the phone company. I was a wire man, Perkowski in the business office, but it helped, being there at the phone company together.

Then six years ago Perkowski and I started Rainbow Cable. We were in on the ground floor of Cable TV. We have the franchises in nine Rhode Island communities, so it's gone well for us. Now and then we're accused of turning it into a club for ex-GI's, but is that so bad? The veterans work hard. They make good team players.

When they call, I try to do right by them. I figure I'm the closest thing to a father some of them have. I reassure them. Yes, they're eligible for membership. Yes, they're welcome at meetings. "The nation is grateful for what you did," I tell them. I try to talk to them the way I wish I had talked to Todd. Why do we learn things after it's too late?

Anyway, when the guy mentioned Todd, I was anxious to hear anything. Sometimes I'll get my wife to call Christina, but you don't want to seem to be prying. The guy said his name was Jesse Binder, said he was on a minesweeper with my son. *USS Impulse*, he called it. He said Todd came aboard for a couple of weeks. "We became like brothers," he said. He said he himself was back home because the mission was complete. The Gulf had been secured. The waters were safe for shipping. "With the Lord's help," he said, "we've pushed them back where they belong."

Nothing on TV looked very secure to me. Hundreds of oil-well fires burned out of control. There were thousands of unexploded mines. "That's only how it looks on the surface," Jesse Binder insisted. "Thank God the major part of the job is done."

I admired his positive attitude. It wasn't until we hung up I realized he hadn't told me that much about Todd.

Two days later he called me again. Had I heard from my son, he wanted to know. He said he was surprised I hadn't, that he expected Todd would call me soon.

He told me, the Lord willing, he would have a job next time we talked. He'd been in the telephone business before he joined the Navy. He was selected for Officer Candidate School, he said, but when the war started he couldn't just sit back and let the other fellow do it all.

"What did you do in the telephone business?" I asked.

"You name it!" he said. "I suppose I've done it all."

"Did you work outside?" I asked.

He wanted to know what I meant by outside.

"Have you done wire?"

"Have I done wire?" he repeated. He said he and another man did an entire subdivision in Houston. "We worked so hard we kept three pole trucks busy," he said. He dreamed about running wire, thought up ways to speed up the process, he said. He thought up ways for the pole crews to go faster. He talked about the Houston project until I finally had to excuse myself.

I didn't ask him about Todd. I hoped he'd say something without my begging for information, but I guess we got talking about his work, and he never got around to Todd.

Meanwhile I was glad to hear Jesse's enthusiasm. I'm not quick to criticize someone who's a little fanatical. In fact, I look for a spark of interest like that, a motivator. I tried to get Todd interested in the cable TV business, but instead he joined the Navy. He could have been in on the ground floor, but I've always said, the main thing is if he's happy.

Of course, now I understand how I felt about Jesse: he seemed to be everything Todd wasn't.

* * * *

I had Jesse come in for an interview, mostly to meet Perkowski. "He comes on a little strong with all the religious talk," said Perkowski, "but hey, as long as you're convinced he knows wire, I guess it's okay."

When I offered Jesse the job he was like a kid — excited, anxious to get to work. He shook my hand in both of his. "The Lord will bless you, Brother Able," he said.

It beat me how Jesse found out about "Able." Actually, my first name *is* "Able," after my grandfather, but everybody calls me Bill. I sign my name "A. William McIntire." Jesse knew things there was no explanation for. He said Able was a good biblical name. He couldn't understand why I didn't like it.

Jesse started with Rainbow Cable the following Monday. I put him with Winston, my most experienced wire man. Winston was Third Armored Cavalry himself. After the first day, he seemed pleased with Jesse's work. "He knows what he's doing around wire," Winston said. "He just won't let you get a word in edgewise."

I laughed. "If you can take it one more day," I said.

Winston shrugged. "It don't really *bother* me," he said. "I just wish there was some way to turn him off." I laughed again. "Hang in there," I told him as he left my office.

The next week went okay, except for a minor snag: Jesse's driver's license was expired. Until he could get a license I put him on DiOrio's truck, working on Rock Creek Manor, a big condo project off Marsh Road in Tiverton. DiOrio was Mister Big Mouth, but a good wire man. I needed him to supervise a crew in Cranston, figured Jesse could take over Rock Creek Manor from him. At lunch break the second day DiOrio dropped Jesse off at the registry to take the driver's exam, then swung by the office. When he stuck his head in my door, I thought it might be about Jesse.

"Thanks a bunch!" he said. "Maybe this afternoon I'll get something done!" I asked what the problem was. "A frigging talking machine," he said. "Does that guy ever quit?" How was he supposed to get any work done with the bible hour going on in his ear? And so on.

DiOrio wasn't known for getting along with people, and I regretted putting Jesse with him. "He's just back from the Gulf," I said. "It's bound to have an effect."

"I understand," said DiOrio. "Just do me a favor and put him on somebody else's truck, will you?"

I told him Jesse would have his own truck by the end of the week, when Coleman started his vacation.

The first week Jesse was on his own, things went great. He was pulling 15 or 16 jobs a day by himself and finishing them all. He came in before eight, pulled his job orders, went right to work. He was the last person to bring his truck in at night. When he rolled in at quarter past five the other wire guys would have already checked out and gone home. If they were still loitering around the platform when they saw Jesse's truck enter the yard, the chit chat would break up in a hurry. "Amen, brother!" they said to one another.

The Tuesday of his second week Jesse was back unexpectedly at 3:45. He had pulled 17 job orders in the morning, but three of the customers were not home, despite being reminded the day before. When this happened to the other wire guys they were glad for an excuse to come in early, but Jesse was steaming.

He stormed into my office, wanted to know who was responsible for making the reminder calls. I tried to calm him down, told him the calls were made, sometimes people just forgot. "It happens, Jesse. We can call them, but we can't make them stay home."

"I guess the Lord put this in my path to test me," he said. He talked about it awhile, gradually calmed down.

But the incident made me uneasy. The angry outburst reminded me of Todd as a teenager. Except Todd usually wanted to get *out* of work. Jesse wanted more. In fact, after that Jesse started pulling 20 job orders in the morning, in case some were not home. But instead of saving the unfinished jobs for the next day, he worked harder, did all 20. Instead of 5:15, his truck started rolling into the yard at 5:45, six o'clock. The dispatcher complained to me about having to stay late, waiting for Jesse. I volunteered to sign him in myself. I never left the office until six-thirty or seven anyway. The dispatcher was grateful. "I just hope you've studied up on your bible," he said.

But Jesse said little to me, just a wave through the window of my office after hanging up his belt. He stopped talking about Todd.

His third week Jesse averaged just under 20 jobs a day. The other wire guys averaged 14, the best among them 16 or 17. I was proud of Jesse, felt my trust had been well placed.

Then the first call came in. Perkowski brought me an address printed on a small slip of paper. "Do you know who did this job?" he asked. Somehow I knew without looking it up, without even knowing why he wanted to know, it would be Jesse.

"Is there a problem?" I asked.

He half shrugged, half laughed. A woman complained the wire man tried to "convert" her. "Best I could tell he wasn't abusive or anything," he said. Perkowski was for calling Jesse on the carpet, setting him straight. "He can't be doing this with customers," Perkowski said. But he never interfered with the wire operations; I never stuck my nose in the administrative stuff.

Of course, I was hung up on Jesse's connection with Todd. I held back, rationalized. I thought, People exaggerate. Who knows what Jesse really said to the woman. She could have been a crank. I worried if I said anything Jesse would take it as anti-religion. I decided to wait, see if it happened again. Well, Perkowski was right.

Before the week was over there was another call. Still, Perkowski left it to me. "I just don't have time to deal with this," he said. I called the man back, an elderly man. He said he believed in God, too, but didn't need a crazy person preaching to him.

"He's a Gulf veteran," I said. A *decorated* Gulf veteran, I added, and he was almost apologetic. I told Linda to screen the calls, give me anything about the wire guys.

The following week there was another call, but I thought I handled it okay. I tried to explain about the stress of being in a war zone. "We're just trying to give this veteran a chance," I said. It got the woman off the line, but I could tell she wasn't exactly happy about it.

Looking back, of course, I should have talked to Jesse about it. Instead I tried being positive. They always said I should have been more positive with Todd. "Why are you always so *negative* with him?" my wife said. So I was positive with Jesse. I was positive about his job. I was positive about how hard he worked. "Nice going, Jesse!" I told him, signing off his installation logs. He was still averaging close to 20 jobs a day.

That was what puzzled me. How could he maintain a pace like that, and still take time to talk all this Jesus talk with customers? Watching Jesse, it was like the Jesus talk got him all pumped up, made him work harder and harder.

My question was: how do you get a kid that fired up over anything? I tried to get Todd interested in Scouts, in model airplanes. Instead he spent his summers hanging out at the lake. He was always a good swimmer, so he took up diving in the Navy. Maybe everybody needs to find his own interests. Maybe with Todd it was diving, with Jesse it was the Jesus scene.

That's the other thing I couldn't figure out: How could these two have been like brothers? To me it didn't seem like Todd, hanging around with a guy like Jesse. And I could never get the straight scoop out of Jesse. Was there anything Todd said to tell us? "He sent his love," Jesse said. "I know he keeps you in his prayers." To me this just wasn't Todd.

Anyway, it was about the fifth week Jesse worked for us. On the sets in the office CNN showed the oil fields burning in Kuwait. Experts from Oklahoma and Texas said it was the worst they'd ever seen.

An oil slick drifted toward the Saudi fresh water plants. On top of that they suspected sabotage at one of the plants. Divers were coming in to inspect the plant's salt water intakes for explosives. I reached to turn up the volume, strained to see if any divers' names were mentioned. Linda at the desk held a phone out to me, but I signaled her to take a message. I watched for 15 minutes, but didn't see Todd, didn't get the name of anyone involved.

Linda had put the message on my desk. I just picked it up when Perkowski came in, handed me another piece of paper. It was the same name on both messages. Woman out in Rock Creek Manor, wanted to know when her installation would be finished. Linda apparently had looked it up, attached the work order. It was marked completed, Jesse's initials on the bottom. I thought of the numbers Jesse was accomplishing — first 18 jobs, then 20, now close to 21 a day. It's a risk you take, I thought. Keeping up that pace, you miss one now and then. But I could handle that. Anybody able to work at twice the speed of my other installers, I could tolerate an occasional slip.

But less than an hour later there was another call. I took it myself. Rock Creek Manor again, this time an older guy. Why was he getting a bill when he had been waiting over a week for the guy to come back and finish? I checked the file myself. But I knew ahead of time it would be one of Jesse's. And when I saw Linda answer the next call I knew. Linda said the woman on the phone called him a Jesus freak. The next caller told me Jesse drilled two holes in her wall, said he'd be back in an hour to lead in the wires. "That was a week and a half ago," she said. She also said a few things about what Rainbow Cable should do if we thought she was paying any bill.

Bills had been mailed the day before, and the calls kept coming in. I spent most of the afternoon on the phone. Eventually Linda stopped writing individual notes, just made a list — name, address, phone number. They were all within a few blocks of one another: all in Jesse's area. On top of all this Perkowski brought me a couple of other names who had insisted on being put through to him. He was good enough just to give me the names, not say anything else.

I waited for Jesse until 5:30. Six o'clock. For a while I tried to do some paperwork, finally went out to a couch in the customer area. I switched between CNN and NBC, but couldn't catch anything on the Saudi fresh water plants. Had they found explosives? Surely it would be over by now, one way or another. I thought of Todd underwater, trying to trace a wire back to its source. What if he pulled the wrong wire? Touched something he shouldn't? How did he know what to touch and what not? They probably didn't even use electric wires any more. Everything nowadays was electronics, remote control.

By then all the other wire men had come and gone. The office was empty. When Jesse's truck was still not back in the yard at 6:15, I drove out to Rock Creek Manor myself.

I hadn't realized how big the development was, and I regretted not having the list with me. I didn't know which houses to check, didn't even know the streets. Plus by now it was dark.

I drove slowly, using the spotlight on my pickup. I had gone a block and a half before I came across a house where the service had been connected. Half a block down there were two more. I got out and checked. The connections looked good. Everything was neat and workmanlike.

But then it was a block before I found another house. It didn't seem right: only four installations in maybe twenty or thirty houses? In most areas our coverage was over fifty percent.

I rang the doorbell at the fourth house. A woman in a purple jump suit greeted me. I told her I was from Rainbow Cable. "Just checking the installation," I told her.

"What installation?" she said.

She showed me where the cable had been brought into the basement, now hung there, the ends taped off. She said the installer told her he had to go back to the shop for additional changers. She'd taken the afternoon off from work to be there for the installer. That was the last she heard. At the next house it was the same story.

I was still trying to work this out in my mind when I spotted Jesse's truck, parked in a driveway, the Rainbow showing up in my headlights.

From the porch I could see the TV in the kitchen. An evangelist gestured from the screen, a large urn of lilies at his side. An elderly woman answered the door. Jesse stood inside by the kitchen table. He didn't have any tools with him.

He introduced me as "Brother Able." She was "Sister Angela." The kitchen table was scattered with pamphlets. *Are You Fulfilling God's Plan?* asked one. The set was tuned to Eternal Life TV. A young preacher in a three-piece suit held his hands on the head of an elderly woman in a wheelchair.

"Sister Angela has just lost her husband," Jesse told me. He told her I too was experiencing sorrow that my son was on a dangerous mission in a foreign land.

"But Brother Able has learned to trust the Lord," he said. The woman looked up at me with tears in her eyes. It seemed she wanted me to say something. Jesse stopped talking and looked at me expectantly. Awkwardly I told her I was sorry about her husband.

"Brother Able's example, his encouragement, it's been an inspiration," Jesse said. He talked about the atmosphere at Rainbow Cable. "You feel God's love surrounding you," he told the woman.

I started to get this feeling of unreality. Was I actually seeing and hearing these things? Was I actually participating in this scene? One thing I knew: Todd would never have gotten mixed up in anything like this.

It was five minutes past seven. On the sink counter a TV dinner was thawing next to the microwave. I tried to bring things to a close, without making a scene. "Well," I said, nodding toward the microwave, "we'd better be leaving you to your dinner."

As we left she hugged Jesse, then turned and hugged me. "I'll pray for your son," she told me.

* * * *

For the next three weeks I put two trucks out in Rock Creek Manor: one to take care of partly finished installations, the other to work on people still waiting to be connected. Perkowski sent a letter of apology to customers. The bills were a computer error, he said. Linda called the people individually, apologized for the inconvenience, offered them a free month of The Home Movie Channel. Thank God none of them went to the Public Utilities Commission. They could have pulled our license just like that. There's three other cable companies around here would *love* to get our franchises.

Of course Perkowski didn't pursue it with me. We know one another well enough. You don't go through life hoping to make no mistakes. You just hope to recover from the ones you make, get on with your business.

In this case, I've pretty much gotten past the whole thing, though I can't help remembering.

It wasn't too bad that night when Jesse and I left Sister Angela's house. I left my pickup there, got Jesse to give me his keys, drove him and his truck back to the shop. All the way back he talked like nothing had changed, like it was business as usual. He said I had been wonderful with Sister Angela.

When we got back to the shop, I told him straight. "It's not working, Jesse," I said. I said he would get two weeks' severance pay that he could pick up his check in the morning. I told him he could count on me for a decent recommendation that I knew he was a good wire man if he put his mind to it. "I'll call it a layoff," I said. "Nobody's fault. Just one of those things."

That night he seemed to take it okay, but the next morning it was a different story. After he got his check from Linda he came to the door of my office, looked directly at me. I stayed behind my desk, not really knowing what to expect. "Even Christ had Judas," he said to me.

I said I was sorry, that there was really no choice. I didn't want to get into it with him. I said I had nothing against him, that I even liked him as a person that I thought he had a lot of promise, and would do well. Still he stared at me. "I hope you don't hold this against me, Jesse, but what else could I have done?" I told him I was finished talking to him, that I needed to get to work. But Jesse was just getting warmed up.

"Now I see," he said. "Now I see what Todd was referring to."

Given the circumstances, I thought I remained pretty cool. I stayed behind my desk, started updating my installation schedule.

"Now I understand what Todd said about you," he said.

"I'm not really interested," I told him. I said if Todd had anything to say he would tell me directly. I said I didn't want to hear any more, and that he could leave.

I guess we were talking louder than I realized, because Perkowski came out of his office. He stood behind Jesse, gently took him by the arm. "It's okay, son," he said. Jesse ignored him, stared at me.

"Now I see," Jesse said. "Now I see what Todd meant." He shrugged off Perkowski's hand. "Todd forgives you," he said. "That's the message: Todd forgives you."

I said I didn't believe it, didn't even believe he knew Todd.

"Tell the old man I forgive him,'" Jesse repeated. "That's what Todd said."

Of course I didn't believe it for a minute. It was just a parting shot. By now Perkowski was turning him around, easing him toward the door. Linda seemed embarrassed. A customer at the front counter gawked at the scene. "God spare you, Brother Able," Jesse called back over his shoulder, "but I forgive you too."

I was okay, actually, but I told Perkowski I was taking the rest of the day off. He said he understood. "Don't let it worry you, Bill," he said. "The guy was a nutball."

"Don't worry," I said. "I'm putting the whole thing behind me."

Mostly I wanted to check with Christina, see if she had heard from Todd. It had been a couple of weeks, she said. No, she couldn't remember Todd talking about anybody named Jesse, or any other really close friends. Certainly no one like a brother to him. "You know Todd," she said, "mostly it's about work." There was a barge stuck on a sand bar, she said. They were trying to use charges to break up the sand bar. "But they have to be careful," Christina said. "They have to be careful," she said, "not to blow a hole in the barge."

I've stopped worrying about the thing with Jesse. Most likely his story was made up, the whole thing about Todd coming aboard the minesweeper Jesse supposedly was on. Thinking back, we never even checked if Jesse was in the Navy, or that he'd been in the Gulf, let alone that he knew Todd. He could have gotten the whole thing out of the newspaper, or talked to somebody in a bar who knew Todd. Anyway, I'll find that out when I talk to Todd.

Of course now there's even talk of bringing Christina and the kids over there. They would give him a condo, a maid, the whole bit, just to keep him over there.

Well, the main thing is if he's happy. Maybe I should let the whole thing drop, just forget about it. If Todd has anything to tell me, he'll tell me himself. He'll tell me when he gets ready to.

Boy in the Wall

Jeremy discovered the black hole while working on Conroy's house, installing insulation for his stepfather. There it was, in the middle of their attic.

He worked Saturdays, crawling in and out of attics. It was his size that made him good for the attics. A month shy of sixteen, just beginning his sophomore year, he was small and thin for his age, more like twelve or thirteen. During the week his stepfather did the side walls. On weekends Jeremy did the attics. Before his stepfather started the insulation business they did trees. His stepfather trimmed what he could reach, left the top branches for Jeremy.

Jeremy had a funny feeling about working on Conroy's house. He was nervous about Mrs. Conroy. Back in middle school she was the school nurse. Jeremy noticed her walking into assembly with the phys ed teacher and the principal the first day. She had light brown hair, down to her shoulders. She wasn't especially tall. She seemed in good shape, like *she* could be the phys ed teacher. But she wasn't like a teacher. She paid attention to kids but didn't give orders in the halls, didn't holler at kids in the cafeteria. She wasn't loud, but kids paid attention to her.

She wasn't like his mother, either. Jeremy watched out for his mother because he didn't know what she might do next. Sometimes when he got home from school, she would just be getting up. Once at three in the afternoon she asked him if he wanted breakfast. His mother complained about being tired, said she gained weight, no matter what. Most likely the medicine she took made her sleepy, made her forget.

His stepfather was big, too. Plus, he had a bad leg, couldn't climb that well. He left the climbing for Jeremy.

The day they did Conroy's house the weather was perfect. Cloudy sky, so it wasn't hot in the attic. The first part of the job was routine. As he unrolled the fiber glass strips, he recognized Mrs. Conroy's voice below. He thought she said something about the apple tree in their back yard.

Every so often she said something else, and he stopped and listened. He couldn't stop too long, of course, or his stepfather started up the ladder to see what was going on. There was always another job waiting. Sometimes they weren't home till after dark.

He knew Mrs. Conroy was the school nurse, married, a mother, but he never thought of her as older. At school she looked at him, always spoke to him. He felt there was something between him and Mrs. Conroy. He would never have told anyone else, but to him she was beautiful.

Once or twice a month in middle school he thought up a reason to go to her office. He was afraid to try this more often. He could fool the teachers, but other kids might see what he was doing, give him a hard time.

Mrs. Conroy listened, took his temperature, gave him aspirin, usually told him to drink a lot of water or juice. She asked him if he ate breakfast. Did he get exercise? Did he have any hobbies? He didn't tell her his hobby was video games.

Jeremy didn't tell his mother he went to the nurse. Once Mrs. Conroy sent a note home with him, something about having his blood levels checked. He threw it in the dumpster behind the grocery. When he left middle school for high school, he hated leaving Mrs. Conroy behind.

He made good time in Conroy's attic until his stepfather stuck his head through the opening, probing with his flashlight. "Where are your gloves?" he asked. "You'll be complaining about your hands."

Jeremy took the two bulky gloves from his hip pocket, brushed his hair back with them, made as if to put them on, until his stepfather climbed back down.

When this job was done, his stepfather would drive straight to the cash machine at the bank, deposit the check. He'd give Jeremy a twenty for his part of the work, then remember something — an errand, an item at the hardware store, a bid on another job. "Take this and run on home," he would tell Jeremy. "Give this to your mother," he would say, handing him another twenty from the stack of bills. "I'll be along as soon as I'm done."

Jeremy saved most of what his stepfather paid him, used some for playing video games. His stepfather said that video games were a waste of time and money. "If you'd only tried that hard at Scouts," he said. Jeremy belonged to Scouts for a year, got as far as Second Class Scout. "Don't quit until you get your First Class," his stepfather told him. "You don't want to end up a second class citizen, do you?"

The Scout troop held a father-son cookout. His stepfather showed up, shook hands all around, talked to the Scoutmaster, while Jeremy arranged the sticks and branches for his fire. "Do you expect that fire to be ready any time tonight?" his stepfather asked — with a big laugh, of course. He said to the Scoutmaster he wished he could get his son to be that careful putting away his things at home.

Sometimes, when his stepfather started in on him, Jeremy imagined video games, played them in his mind. He tried to teach this trick to his sister, Elizabeth, but it didn't work for her. She took their stepfather too seriously, didn't know how to stay out of his way. At least his stepfather never beat Elizabeth. Jeremy saved some extra money and bought her a pocket-sized radio, so she would have something to do, something to take up her attention.

He discovered the black hole when he was finishing the Conroy job. He couldn't see the bottom. It was just a small open space, straight down into the center of the house. It was like it was left over when the builder finished, and they didn't know what to put there. He lay on his stomach, put his face down in the hole. It was still and warm there. He thought he smelled meat cooking. Even after his eyes adjusted he saw nothing.

"What's taking you so long up there?" his stepfather called from the garage. "Aren't you finished yet?" Jeremy didn't answer. With his head in the hole, sounds were distant and muffled. He wondered how deep the hole was. "What have you been doing all this time?" his stepfather called out. When he heard his stepfather close the tool box, he quickly finished up. As he tucked in the last piece of insulation, his stepfather was already back on the ladder, inspecting the job.

Jeremy said nothing to his stepfather, but he thought about it on the way home. He wondered what was at the bottom of the hole, wondered if he could stand up in it. He wondered if he could reach the bottom.

* * * *

On Sunday his mother still slept as he got dressed. He didn't know where his stepfather was. Elizabeth sat on the sofa in her pajamas, watching a cartoon about teenagers. He told her there were donuts left from Saturday, asked if she wanted one.

"Where are you going?" she asked.

"Who said I'm going anywhere?" he said. "Anyway, don't worry. I'll be back." Sometimes he worried about Elizabeth. What would happen to her? Would she grow up to be like their mother? Would she sleep all the time? What would happen to her kids?

He went straight to Conroy's street, waited out of sight down the block until their car passed, taking them to church, Mr. and Mrs. in front, their daughter Karen in back. He slipped in through the garage, by ten after nine he was looking into the hole again. This time he lowered himself into the hole feet first. When his feet touched bottom his head was a foot below the surface of the attic. Around him on all sides he felt wallboard. He sat on a small ledge formed by a joist running through one side of the black hole.

Sunday morning, the neighborhood was quiet. He thought of Mrs. Conroy at church, head and eyes lowered in prayer. In the car she looked dressed up. In school even when it was bad weather she looked nice. *Hi, Jeremy! Some weather! Don't your feet get cold in those sneakers?*

Besides visits to her office, he talked to Mrs. Conroy one other time in middle school. On vaccination day, she stuck his finger to get a blood sample. That day she wore a yellow sun dress. Her hair just touched the thin straps over her sun-tanned shoulders. He liked the feel of her hand holding his finger. Now he wondered how much Mrs. Conroy remembered about him. Did she know he installed the insulation in her attic?

By the time he boosted himself out of the hole he heard cars in the street. It was later than he realized. In another minute car doors slammed. They were back from church. He felt weak, in a panic. They passed through the garage, Karen saying something about her girl friend's scarf. Evidently Mr. Conroy didn't notice any sign that he had passed through the garage getting into the attic. Mrs. Conroy's heels clicked on the garage floor, then on the kitchen floor.

For a few minutes he froze to the spot. A door closed. He waited for minutes, listened. The kitchen door opened and closed. He didn't know who was out and who was in. Afraid to leave, he crawled back to the hole, lowered himself in. He felt safe inside the hole. Nearby, through the wall, someone turned on a radio, tuned it past choirs and Sunday preachers, finally stopped at a classical station.

He smelled bacon and coffee, heard silverware, plates, the Conroys eating breakfast. Earlier he had a donut, but by now he felt hungry again. He couldn't make out words, but he could tell voices apart. Mrs. Conroy sounded calm, just like she had at school. *Does your throat feel sore? Did you have breakfast this morning?* He thought of Mrs. Conroy in her Sunday clothes. He wondered if she had changed, what she wore now.

The dishwasher started. The TV came on — a football game. Jeremy felt peaceful. He sat on the ledge, his knees resting against the opposite wall. Eventually he found he could curl up at the bottom of the hole. It felt like his own place.

Outside on the street he heard kids playing. He understood only a few words from the house around him, but he followed the Conroys through their Sunday afternoon and evening, imagined the rooms they were in, what they were doing. But he didn't recognize some of the TV programs they watched.

Once he heard Mrs. Conroy's voice nearby, just on the other side of the wall. It was onesided, a telephone conversation. She sounded only two or three feet away. He felt himself breathing faster. Once at school she slid the back of his shirt up, listened to his lungs with a stethoscope. *Okay, now, Jeremy, a deep breath?* He fell asleep remembering this, slept through the entire night.

* * * *

When he woke up next morning the Conroys were already moving around. He stood up, stretched his legs and feet, wiggling his toes to get the circulation going. Now and then Mrs. Conroy called reminders to the others. Doors opened and closed, cars started. He heard kids' voices, thought he heard Karen laugh when the school bus stopped for her. Mrs. Conroy must have already gone. After things were quiet he lifted himself out of the hole and left.

On the way out he smelled perfume, where Mrs. Conroy had passed. It smelled like spices. The scent frightened him, but he was excited, too. It created a forbidden atmosphere, almost a forbidden touch. He liked the dangerous feeling of this atmosphere. He didn't want to lose it.

He tied his sweatshirt around his waist, set off down the street like a jogger. He headed for the mall, disappeared among the crowds until three-thirty, when he figured Mrs. Conroy would be home for the day.

* * * *

Jeremy felt nervous ringing the doorbell, but Mrs. Conroy smiled when she answered. "Jeremy!" she said. She treated him like an old friend.

"Hello, Mrs. Conroy," he said. He looked away, toward the trees, stuck his hands in the pockets of his jeans. "I came to ask if I could rake your leaves," he said. *Do you know we live in the same house?* he thought.

She said Mr. Conroy had a riding mower, that he *liked* doing leaves. "If I gave his job away," she said, "he would never forgive me."

Jeremy felt foolish, tried not to show it. He shrugged, started to turn and go.

She put a hand on his arm. "It's so good to see you, Jeremy," she said. She told him Mr. Conroy was pleased with the insulation job. "I didn't realize it was you," she said, "until you were finished and gone. Karen told me it was Elizabeth's brother." She looked at him as if trying to see inside him. "You must be keeping busy," she said. "All the work for your father...Now doing leaves." He wanted to stay there with her hand on his arm. *How long has your arm hurt?* he wanted to hear her say. *You should put heat on it,* she could say. *Do you have a heating pad at home?*

All he could think of was to tell her yes, that he was pretty busy. "Thanks," he said, and started back down the walk.

For a few seconds he felt her looking at the back of his neck, until he heard the door close.

After dark Jeremy returned, stood behind a tree next to Conroy's driveway. A television flickered behind the living room drapes. Jeremy thought he heard Karen's music from deeper inside the house.

He slipped into the garage, shimmied back into the attic with hardly a sound.

* * * *

He was awake a lot during the night, going over things Mrs. Conroy said, what they meant. She seemed glad to see him. When she touched his arm, it was like middle school, in the nurse's office. Every time he woke up during the night he felt her fingers on his arm.

Next morning after everyone cleared out, Jeremy let himself out through the garage again. He spent the day at the mall, thinking of what to say when he came back at three-thirty.

At the mall, a girl sitting by the fountain got up and talked to Jeremy. Her hair and makeup made her look older, but when he talked to her he could see she was his age. "Where are you from?" she said. She laughed when he said he lived a mile away. She said she was from Michigan. Jeremy was surprised: he wondered where she actually *lived*, where she stayed at night.

"You can always find someplace to stay," she said, "something to eat." She dug cigarettes out of a blue knapsack, offered one to Jeremy, but he didn't want to smell like cigarettes when he talked to Mrs. Conroy.

Then the girl asked Jeremy for money. He gave her two dollars in quarters he found in his pocket.

* * * *

When Mrs. Conroy answered the door that afternoon Jeremy tried to look directly at her. She smiled at him, said his name. But was she more serious than the day before? She looked almost worried, like she didn't know what to say. Like she wanted to tell him something, but couldn't. He had never seen her at a loss for words.

"I'm sorry to bother you again, Mrs. Conroy," he said. He told her he did other work, besides leaves; he fixed things; painted; did errands.

He didn't know what to say next. Something about leaves? About the riding mower? Then he remembered the apple tree. "October," he said. "It's the right time of year to prune it, trim it up for next year."

They walked around to the back yard to look at it. "It's an old tree, Jeremy," she said. "I'm not sure it can take pruning."

He told her the tree was killing itself, that it needed to be thinned out. He showed her places where branches rubbed against each other, causing the tree to bleed.

That seemed to convince her. She brought him a small saw and a pair of pruning shears.

Standing on the ground, he did the lower branches. He handled each branch carefully. Where two of them twined together, threatened to strangle one another, he separated them with his fingers, trimmed them back. He picked the few remaining apples as he worked, gathered another three or four from the ground, lined them up on Conroy's back steps. He climbed into the tree, cut out dead branches, thinned others. The last apple was near the top, a real prize, twice the size of his fist, deep red from catching the sun. It wouldn't fit in his pocket, so he tucked it inside his shirt before he climbed down.

When he finished he rang the doorbell. He handed Mrs. Conroy the prize apple, showed her the others on the steps. She seemed delighted, held the apple up and admired it. She told him how much better the tree looked, said what a good job he'd done. "Jeremy," she said, "I'm amazed at all your talents."

Jeremy had never thought of tree work as a talent. "It will have room to breathe now," he said.

She said she would save a jar of applesauce for him.

Jeremy didn't hear the truck drive up. His stepfather was already out, coming up the driveway. He glanced at Jeremy.

"Just wanted to make sure everything was okay," he told Mrs. Conroy. "Get in the truck," he told Jeremy.

Mrs. Conroy said her husband was pleased with the insulation. She also said Jeremy had done a great job on their apple tree.

"I'll bet he did," said his stepfather. He took Jeremy's sleeve, led him down the driveway to the truck. Jeremy didn't hear anything else Mrs. Conroy said. When his stepfather took him, her expression changed. Something went out of her face, out of her eyes. It was almost like *she* needed help, needed him to do something.

She stayed in the driveway until they drove off. But Jeremy couldn't look at her. Couldn't even say goodbye.

* * * *

After his stepfather finished with him, Jeremy went to his room and stayed there. He didn't come out for supper. He heard the TV with his stepfather's evening shows. On TV there was sporadic gunfire. Cars or speedboats roared around. Someone shouted an order, and they roared off again.

The TV stopped abruptly in the middle of a commercial. Neither of his parents said anything, but he heard them go to bed.

Jeremy stayed awake, thinking of Mrs. Conroy. He felt his arm where she touched him two days before. He thought of her expression in the driveway, of being in her attic, hearing her voice on the other side of the wall. *I'm amazed at all your talents,* she told him.

He dozed off and dreamed. In his dream he was back in Conroy's attic, in the black hole. In his dream it was dark, and before he realized, the space became smaller. Closed in on him. Mrs. Conroy was on the other side of the wall. Telling him to get out. He was held all around, his arms pinned to his sides. *Jeremy...* he heard her say. He tried to answer. Couldn't speak. *Jeremy...* she called after him.

The walls crushed his shoulders, his arms, his hips. He felt everything turn over. Blood rushed to his head. She couldn't reach him. He couldn't reach her.

Did he actually struggle? Or was this part of the dream? Struggling to breathe, he finally freed his head. Then he forced his shoulders out, soon had his arms unstuck. With a massive lurch he floated free, weightless, in the middle of space. Waking like that, exhausted, he felt as if he'd finished a day's work, completed something; survived some awful accident.

When the turmoil of the dream died down, he realized the house was still and dark around him. Outside his window it wasn't as dark as he'd thought it would be. The neighborhood was quiet. He got dressed, putting on an extra shirt. Over his jacket he put on his parka, even though it was only October. He stuffed extra underwear and socks into the parka pockets. He still had the money Mrs. Conroy gave him, more he'd saved from insulation jobs. Downstairs he found Elizabeth's tape player, folded a bill and tucked it inside the case. He had enough left for a bus ticket, and then some. And there were places to stay, Jeremy thought, places to get something to eat.

On his way out he took his stepfather's pruning shears off the garage wall and zipped them in his parka. On the empty hook he hung his insulation gloves.

Out in the street he looked back at the house. It was like the others in the neighborhood — dim, grayish-green shapes.

It was still dark when he cut through Conroy's back yard one last time. He looked up at their roof, their attic. It too was like other houses around it, now in sharper contrast to the lightening sky.

He ducked under the apple tree. The grass was wet. His foot hit something — a last apple he'd missed. He dried it off on his shirt, started to put it on their back steps, then changed his mind, stuck it in his parka pocket and headed down the street.

The Walk Will Do Them Good

"He writes poetry and likes sports!" my daughter said. "You'll love him, Daddy," she told me. All the while my wife is giving me this look that says, *Don't disappoint her!*

This all developed since she insisted on moving into her own apartment, took half the house furniture with her, including my end table that held my lamp and my newspaper.

My wife gave me forty-five minutes of instruction on how to behave when they came over for Sunday dinner. But didn't mention this guy's blond hair down to his shoulders. Or that he was 35 if a day. Or that his sport was squash. Or about the motorcycle, my daughter hanging on in back like she didn't have good sense.

So, *Fine!* I shook hands, kept my mouth shut, did the barbecue, smiled when everybody else did, answered if spoken to. Then before things got too chummy, before my daughter's baby pictures and this guy's notebook of poems were passed around, I made my joke about air pollution, took my cigar and coffee out in the front yard. Took a good look at this guy's Japanese motorcycle.

All in all, I thought, my wife could be proud of me. I didn't ask who he voted for or what church he went to; or if he'd ever had a real job; or if he'd been married; or why he kept referring to "our" apartment.

I didn't ask if he knew the first thing about motorcycles; or what would happen if there was half a cup of coffee in his gas tank, and he drove it that way.

So, *Fine!* Maybe he'll learn something; maybe they both will. Whatever. The walk will do them good.

The Mysterious Survival of Lawrence Tubb

Eighth grade ended on a bad note, a member of the class shot and killed in an accident just before graduation. The death clouded our last few weeks of school, hung like a mist over our commencement Mass. It shows in the class picture: lined up on the front steps of church, my classmates and I look serious and preoccupied. We were anxious to get out of there, get on to summer vacation and high school.

I could never seem to be able to put eighth grade behind me. Sometimes I've wondered if what happened then held me back in some mysterious way: when I dropped out of law school after a semester; when I was turned down for promotion to manager. Twenty-five years later, it was still a bad memory, and I was surprised to receive the invitation: *St. Anthony's School Reunion, 1981-2006.* I wouldn't have thought our class wanted a reunion.

I showed my wife the letter, signed *Your Class President and Reunion Chairman, L. Almon Tubb.* My wife was from another town, so the name didn't ring a bell with her — even though I'd told her the story. Actually, Linda was my third wife, a hostess I met on a trip through Connecticut. Don't get me wrong, my wife is a good woman. But add marriage to my list of failures. Put it at the top of the list, ahead of law school.

"L. Almon" was news to me — back then his name was Larry. We called him "Tubby." He was the fattest kid in St. Anthony's school. Fattest, least popular, the most completely out of it.

After graduation he disappeared, sent off to prep school, I presume college. Actually, he was sick the last month of eighth grade — sort of a nervous breakdown — didn't graduate with the class. Maybe he was given a diploma in absentia, I don't remember. How he became "Class President and Reunion Chairman" I have no idea.

But the invitation was like a challenge: would I have the guts to show up? My relationship with Tubby — I hate to even call it that — what went on between Tubby and me wasn't pretty.

Did Tubby remember it? Or were the memories yet to come? Would he wake up some night, as I have a dozen times, with the whole thing staring me in the face? Camel carrying the crucifix, looking down at me, knowing everything that went on. If Tubby remembered it, how did he get past it, get on with his life? How did he get beyond it all, when I was still stuck in the same rut twenty-five years later?

For a few months in eighth grade Donny DePriest and I hung out with Tubby. His father owned the Chevrolet and Buick dealerships in town. The family had money, and their house was bigger than any in St. Anthony parish, set back from the others, on a winding driveway, at the edge of the woods which surrounded the town. The rest of us at St. Anthony's were working-class kids. My father was a machinist at the parts factory; Donny's — when he was sober — painted houses.

Tubby was an only child, had a room to himself, on the second floor, looking into the woods. There was actually a balcony outside Tubby's room. When Donny and I played gangster at Tubby's, we always made Tubby be the straight guy, bound and gagged, bent back over the rail of the balcony with a gun to his nose. Tired of that, we ridiculed the voices he picked up on short wave radio, threatened to disfigure his expensive baseball card collection unless he became a Red Sox fan.

In the basement was a complete model railroad, trains running through towns with houses and stores and flickering lights. Donny and I tried to cause collisions, but trains on the same track magically slowed before overtaking one another.

We became interested in shooting after we exhausted other possibilities. Tubby's father was a world-class outdoorsman, had a lodge on a big private lake in Canada. Each year he chartered a seaplane to bring his top corporate customers there for the start of the hunting season.

Tubby was not yet invited to hunt at the lodge, but his father bought him a pellet gun we shot off his balcony into the woods, pinging a transformer on the telephone pole. Tubby's shooting was weak and indecisive. Of course we taunted him about that. "How come if your father is such a hot-shot hunter you can't hit diddly?"

I sometimes wondered, why does he take it? Why does he let Donny and me play at his house? His mother or the maid would greet us at the door like we were the family's favorite cousins. "Larry's waiting for you upstairs," they said. Still, we treated him as our flunky or slave or prisoner of war or whatever.

Only once did we get in trouble at Tubby's house. Mister Tubb's den was upstairs. We weren't supposed to go in there, but one day we pressured Tubby into taking us. It was a room with dark paneling, framed black and white photographs of moose and caribou in the wild, stuffed and mounted rainbow trout and bass from Canada. There was an autographed picture of Governor Slocum in Mister Tubb's boat, netting what must have been a 15-pound pike. In the corner was a polished mahogany desk, a matching liquor cabinet and a wet bar. In a case on the wall were displayed Mister Tubb's five or six guns.

From this inner sanctum a hidden staircase led to somewhere in the rear of the first floor. The maid heard us — who knows, in *that* house there may even have been an alarm. She came up the hidden staircase to nail us in the act.

That evening our parents were called, and we were summoned back to the Tubb house to receive a lecture from Mister Tubb himself. From then on we stayed out of his den, that is until that last day.

* * * *

Out of 25 in our class, 16 showed up for the reunion, a good turnout, considering three had died. Roy Barkley died in Marine boot camp — some undetected heart defect. Dolores DiVicenzo told me Cindy Kemper got ovarian cancer when she was thirty-five, didn't live to her thirty-sixth birthday. The other was Camel Cardoza, killed accidentally the month before graduation.

Camel was older than the rest of us, held back a couple of grades before they finally defaulted him through the system. He was constantly in trouble with the nuns, a couple of times with the police. He wore a pack of Camels rolled up in his T-shirt sleeve, more than once showed up at school that way. Sister Felicitas confiscated the cigarettes and gave them to the Hmong refugee janitor. Camel was the only boy in eighth grade whose stage of puberty matched that of the girls. Some of the girls even seemed to think he was exciting.

Still, he ignored us all, was contemptuous of the boys, accused us of having no sex organs. He swore with a facility that made us jealous, using words that sent us to the dictionary. He accused

Lo Wat, the janitor, of stealing his cigarettes, was about to take him apart before Sister Felicitas separated them. For the most part Camel came and went as he pleased. Sister Felicitas was the only person with any control over him. She got him to receive Communion with the rest of the class on First Fridays and every Wednesday during Lent and Advent. On these class Communion days there was hot chocolate and doughnuts afterward in the lunch room, and Camel loitered over his two doughnuts at a corner table, sometimes not showing up in the classroom until 9:30 or 10:00, if at all.

I was afraid of Camel, after an incident early in the year. I came across him smoking in the boys' room. When Sister Felicitas smelled the smoke and confronted him, Camel thought I told her. He didn't accuse me directly, but held me in a head lock in the cloak room for an entire lunch period. After that he took every opportunity to trap me in the stalls in the boys' room, threatened to flush me down a toilet.

* * * *

Tubby was involved in the accident that killed Camel. Donny and I were involved, too, indirectly, and maybe that's what hung over me all those years. When Tubby disappeared at the end of eighth grade, I never expected to see him again. I thought our bullying of Tubby, which culminated in the accident, might have wrecked his life, sent him into seclusion. Over the years I rationalized it: I was only a kid; I couldn't have known what would happen; and so on. But now and then, when memories surfaced, I felt guilty.

That made it even more of a shock to see his name on the reunion invitation. But what really set me back the night of the reunion was his appearance. When he greeted Linda and me I honest-to-God didn't recognize him. For starters, he wasn't fat any more. Most of us were doing our best to suck it in so we could button our sports coats. But Tubby was fit, slender, and sun-tanned.

"You old son of a gun," he shouted, crushing my hand in his. He turned to Linda. "How did a good-looking woman like you get mixed up with this reprobate?" he asked, hugging me in a muscle-bound vice of fine wool and expensive cologne.

He reached into a crowd of people behind him and pulled out a grinning Donny DePriest, already into what seemed to be his third or fourth vodka. "Get a picture of this, Hon!" Tubby shouted at his wife, hugging Donny with one arm, me with the other. "The three musketeers!" he announced to everyone within hearing.

Naturally his wife was beautiful, sexy, bright, and classy. Tubby said he had "given up" his father's Buick and Chevrolet dealerships, moved to Philadelphia, that he was selling produce. "Lettuce and tomatoes," he said, with a laugh, turning to greet a new arrival. Donny DePriest told me about Almon-Della Produce, truck terminals up and down the entire Atlantic seaboard. "He supplies the fresh salad greens for every major hotel chain east of the Mississippi," Donny said.

Donny was with a woman I didn't know, a dark-haired waif of a person who sipped a bottomless glass of sherry. Donny himself was drinking vodka like soda pop. He had divorced his first wife eight years before, he said. He had a daughter in the community college; a son on a Patrol Frigate in the Persian Gulf.

Neither of us talked about eighth grade, the things we both must have been thinking, about what happened that April before graduation. It took place on Holy Thursday, three days before Easter. We were out of school, but had to appear that evening to sing the marathon Holy Thursday services, march in the procession. After two days of rain, the baseball diamond was a lake. Donny and I loitered all morning outside Zimmerman's Super Market, split a half gallon of RC Cola and a family-size bag of potato chips. Then Donny suggested we head for Tubby's, to get in some target practice.

We took our usual short cut through an alley lined with board fences. We kicked the fences and rickety garage doors, stirring up every dog in the neighborhood. As we passed the last garage, Camel Cardoza emerged through the back gate.

When he saw us he seemed to sense an opportunity. "What are you two wimps doing?" he said.

"Nothing," I answered, at the same time Donny — apparently wanting to impress Camel — explained about the target practice off Tubby's balcony. Knowing Camel, I felt things starting to go downhill. I wanted to call the whole thing off, told Donny I didn't really want to shoot, that I had to be home, anyway. Camel wouldn't have it. "You can't wimp out *now*," he said, taking my arm. "You ask me to come back here and shoot with you, and now you want to wimp out?" He twisted my arm behind my back, forcing me up the gravel driveway to Tubby's house.

This day Tubby answered the door himself. It was the maid's day off, and Mrs. Tubb was on the altar committee, busy at church with Holy Thursday preparations. Tubby seemed delighted to see Camel, treated him like a celebrity, gave him a complete tour of the house, demonstrating all his toys and gadgets. Camel watched the electric train in silence, flicking cigarette ashes into a waste can in the corner. "You got a nice layout here, Lawrence," he said. Like Sister Felicitas, Camel used Tubby's full given name.

It was the same with the short wave radio and the baseball card collection. Camel let Tubby have center stage, listened attentively to garbled French Tubby said was Montreal. All the while Camel kept his eye on Donny and me. If we didn't show enough appreciation of Tubby's various possessions, most of which we had grown tired of, Camel made derogatory remarks about our understanding of what we were seeing.

"You're amazing, Lawrence," he said. "You understand all this shit. That's something."

Tubby beamed, soaking up the attention. I wanted only to get out of the house somehow, to disengage from Camel. But he insisted we all go up to Tubby's room and shoot. "Especially since you two are such hot shits," he said to Donny and me.

When Tubby held the refrigerator door open for us, Camel regarded it thoughtfully, but declined. Tubby, for the first time I remembered, didn't take a snack either. Donny seemed about ready to reach for an eclair, but I pinched him in the elbow. "Nothing for me, thanks," I said.

I had to go to the bathroom before we shot, but Camel wouldn't have it. "Don't turn this weirdo loose in your bathroom," he said to Tubby. "He'll probably steal the soap." We all laughed, but I knew better than to try to go.

I expected Camel to make fun of the pellet gun. Instead he admired it, handled it like something fit for a gun collector, testing the weight, the grip, sighting down the barrel. Then he handed the gun to Tubby. "Okay, Lawrence," he said. "Show these wimps what you can do."

Tubby, usually erratic, somehow hit the transformer box on the telephone pole with a solid ping on his first shot. Like an idiot, Donny also scored on his first shot. Wiggly from having to pee, wanting the whole thing over, I fired into the sky above the pole.

Camel snickered as I gave the gun to him. He passed it straight to Tubby. "Okay, Lawrence," he said. "You're hot. You shoot for me." Confident, now, Tubby took the gun, raised it to his shoulder, miraculously pinged the box a second time.

Donny reached for the gun but Camel took it. "Lawrence here has a higher score than both you wimps put together," he said. Tubby seemed pleased, but asked Camel if we didn't get another turn. "Don't worry about it, Lawrence," Camel said. "DePriest here got lucky," he said in Donny's direction. Then he gestured toward me with the gun. "And this big baby is about to pee his pants."

Camel handed the air rifle back to Tubby. "Isn't your father a hunter?" he said. "Let's take a look at some *real* guns."

I couldn't believe it when Tubby led the three of us to the den. He went straight to the gun case on the wall, took down one of his father's shotguns, held it out to Camel.

With the gun in his hands Camel was transformed. He aimed it out the window, aimed it at each of the wildlife photographs, aimed it at the governor, aimed it at my private parts.

I felt like I was going to go right in my pants. "Hey, no kidding," I said. "I really have to piss."

"You wimp," Camel said. "Go on home to your Mommy." He aimed the gun at Donny. "And take your weird friend with you."

Donny and I ran into each other getting out the door. I pushed him out first, thought for a second of using the bathroom back in Tubby's room, but was afraid Camel might change his mind about letting us go. Donny was halfway down the stairs, and I followed.

Outside, breathing hard, we tried to make a joke of it. "Fucking Camel!" I said.

"That Cardoza is *crazy!*" Donny said. He yelped and laughed nervously, looking back toward the house.

"Wait till Felicitas hears about *this!*" I said.

We stopped to take a leak behind the hedge along Tubb's driveway, had just zipped up when we heard the shot from the house. Donny made a small high sound, I jumped, then we both started to run. We took out together across the street, turned down the alley toward our homes, ran all the way, dogs barking on either side of us. At the end of the alley Donny turned toward his house, still running. I ran toward mine, without a word.

After that our parents forbade us to hang out with each other. We went to different high schools. I got a business degree at Bryant, Donny started on the night shift at Brown and Williamson. Soon we lost contact.

* * * *

The reunion went as reunions do: mostly drinking and bragging. Except it was Tubby's show from the beginning. He commanded the scene, welcomed new arrivals, hugged the wives. When it came time for dinner, he was Master of Ceremonies.

To say grace he introduced a new young pastor, who seemed deferential to him. Tubby kept all the nearby wine glasses filled, summoned waiters and waitresses for his classmates at other tables, told stories in between. After dinner Tubby handed out the prizes for the most children, the longest married, the farthest distance traveled. He had personal stories about everyone, recalled incidents I had long forgotten from our eight years at St. Anthony's. A stranger would have thought he had been the class personality, the student voted most likely to succeed.

It gave an unfamiliar texture to the evening, as if I'd come to the wrong reunion at the wrong school, or fallen in with a class other than my own. It gave my own recollection of that Holy Thursday an unfamiliar feel, as if I'd imagined it all. I wanted to talk to Donny, get him to corroborate my memories. But he was getting drunker as the evening wore on, and it seemed Tubby was always between us, clapping us both on the shoulders, recalling something from our collective childhood.

* * * *

Probably because she knew he wouldn't sing with the rest of us, Sister Felicitas assigned Camel to dress in choir robes and carry the cross at the front of processions. Though he was the cross-bearer in the daily practices, he rarely showed up for the ceremony. "I had to work," he said. Or: "My grandmother was sick." Sometimes we heard him give one excuse to Sister Felicitas, a different one to the music teacher.

That Holy Thursday night, with Tubby and Camel both absent, Sister Felicitas took me by the shoulder, had me carry the cross in place of Camel. Others moved up to fill the spot vacated by Tubby.

The six o'clock local news had shown an ambulance pulled up to Tubby's house, attendants carrying out a stretcher with a body bag. *Sixteen-year-old Rafael Cardoza,* the account said, *was shot and killed by a blast from a 40-gauge shotgun he was examining at the home of a friend, Lawrence Tubb, 13, of Valley Vista Road. The boys were alone in the house at the time.*

For Camel's funeral all the eighth-grade boys put on shirts and ties, suits or sport coats if they had them. Tubby walked between his parents. His mother was swathed in black and heavily veiled. Afterward she embraced Mrs. Cardoza and the grandmother and Maria Cardoza, Camel's sister, a thin fourth grader. Mister Tubb, in tailored pin stripes, shook hands with Mister Cardoza, who breathed heavily in a suit too small for him.

The larger boys carried the casket; I straggled along behind with the others. In the paper my name was accidentally omitted from the list of participants. I imagined the newsman sensed how I tried to avoid being near Camel's body. Years later I wondered if anyone connected me with the shooting, perhaps held me somehow responsible.

* * * *

By the time the reunion banquet wound down, Donny was slumped in his chair, across the table from me, on the verge of nodding off. He and his date and Linda and I were the only two couples at a table for eight. I wondered if others knew how Donny and I treated Tubby, knew how Camel ended up in Tubby's house that afternoon.

Time for the final invocation, the young priest had retired, Tubby handled the prayers himself. He prayed for our deceased parents and relatives, the priest who had been our old pastor, nuns who had passed away in the intervening years. Then, in solemn tones, he remembered "the three deceased members of our class, now gone to their eternal rewards." Donny made a noise, stirred in his seat.

There was a collective intake of breath when Tubby started to name our classmates who had died. He referred to Roy Barkley as "a valiant Marine, a hero."

"*A-men!*" said Donny, too loud. He was suddenly awake, looking at Tubby, eyes glazed with tears. Donny's date patted his hand. Several people at the next table looked in our direction.

Meanwhile Tubby continued with the prayer, called Cindy Kemper "a courageous victim of a dread disease."

"God bless her!" said Donny. He scraped his chair back from the table, to face the podium directly. Again people at the next table stirred uneasily. I was embarrassed, felt the blood rise in my face.

In the pause that followed, Tubby looked out at us, scanned each table, as if looking for someone to provide the name of the third deceased.

"Rafael…Cardoza," Tubby said, looking over our heads, into the shadows at the back of the hall.

Donny whispered "Camel" to his date, loud enough for people around us to hear.

At the podium, Tubby went on. "Rafael Cardoza," he said, and paused again. Donny started to rock forward, trying to stand up from the table. His date put a hand on his arm.

"Given the chance," Tubby continued, "given the opportunity, Rafael Cardoza would have surpassed us all."

In the hush that followed, Donny lurched out of his chair with his hand raised, as if to address the gathering. But he seemed unable to choose among the emotions flooding him. "Camel!" he said finally, looking around the room for agreement. "We called him Camel, right?" He wiped away tears with one hand. His date tried to coax him back into his seat. People kept their heads bowed.

At the podium, Tubby raised a hand in benediction. "God bless you, Donny," he said. "Thank you for sharing that. We all remember." But while he addressed Donny, Tubby's gaze rested on me, the beginning of an ironic smile at the corners of his mouth. "We all remember, Donny," he said. "Yes, we do." Then, after a brief silence, he added, "In Jesus' name," and everyone exhaled an emphatic "*Amen!*"

Donny stayed on his feet for a few seconds, then started to waver. Somebody helped me get him onto a couch at the side of the room, while his date went after their coats. Except for a few sidelong glances, people ignored him as the program came to an end.

The entire business left me depressed for weeks, embarrassed by my childhood memories, embarrassed by what happened at the party, embarrassed by my own mediocre accomplishments in life. And jealous: jealous of Tubby, jealous of Donny's immunity from it all, jealous even of the long-departed Camel.

That night I stood there in a daze, watched my classmates flock around Tubby. They hugged him, wished him well, thanked him. Someone called it "a healing experience." I was swept to the side, unable to respond, unable even to say goodbye.

Instead I turned my attention to getting Linda's coat. She was trying to show me a type of drape they had there in the banquet hall, for keeping out heat, or keeping it in. And there was no talking to Donny, who slept peacefully as we carried him to his car.

Finish Man

This is about loyalty and skill and hard work: is it worth it? From the way I've been treated these last few days — you wonder!

I've been Lenny Ribeiro's finish man the last four years. I'm your top finish man in Bristol County. Top carpenter, for that matter. Cabinets, doors, counter tops: you name it. It's second nature. More than that, I've had plenty to offer Lenny himself: how he could improve his business, ways he could get ahead. But what have I got to show for it? You wonder what being top *anything* gets you.

One thing: to be successful I don't need Lenny or anybody else. It wouldn't take me anything to be on my own if I wanted, clear 100 grand a year, easy. But who needs the hassle? If you saw Lenny, you'd know what I mean. He's on the job at 7:45, same as me, plus he has all the owners to deal with: what doors they want, where they want the built-ins, what colors the wife wants, and so on. Any complaints, rework, breakage, all goes straight to Lenny. He has all the scheduling, has to check out the work when it's done. He has the vendors: why didn't this get delivered? Why has such and such gone up a dollar? Also, what if it rains?

We knock off, Lenny's back in his office in the trailer, picking up his phone messages. By five-thirty every night I'm settled down on my favorite stool in Charlie's. Mike McCorkle is always there, Dennis, Billy the Accountant, Donna and Rita, the other girls. You should see Charlie's the night of any Bruins game: Talk about *noise!* Talk about *electricity!* Guys giving high fives for every Bruins' goal! Last time they made the finals, Rita is up dancing on the bar!

Meanwhile Lenny's home making his phone calls, trying to collect his money, arranging start-ups for the next day. I'm sorry: that's not for me. The way I look at it, I don't work for Lenny, Lenny works for me: he's like my agent. I should say *was* my agent. I had to quit yesterday afternoon. You can only take so much.

Anyway, I don't hold hard feelings. After all, I've been with Lenny nine years, five as regular carpenter, the last four as finish man. Lenny isn't a bad builder. Like I said, he works hard. But the man is stressed out. He'll regret what happened.

The first five years, I was out on the job with everybody else. I broke in a lot of the new guys, showed them what they were doing wrong. I believe in helping a young guy get off on the right foot, so if I see something, I tell them. I say: Why hold back? Lenny, too, for that matter: I was always open with Lenny, willing to suggest how he might improve things.

And let's face it: we did good! Throwing up condos as fast as you could haul lumber. Mostly we built for Cabral, one of the biggest developers around. East Bay, Sakonnet Village, Cedar Farm — those were all Cabral's.

Personally, I liked Cabral. He drove a yellow Cadillac, but you could tell by his hands: he was strictly a hard-hat. He came out on the job, checked things out. I've had many's the cup of coffee with Cabral, right on site, gave him a few pointers on places to look at, possible investments.

Got so when he came on site I knew he'd like to get together with me, but held back because of the other guys. So when his Cadillac pulled up I'd make it over there to pick up a tool or something, just in case he wanted to talk.

I don't blame the other guys for being jealous. Most of them grew up not knowing that much to begin with, which accounts for a lot of the mentality I have to deal with. "Hey, Mister Wall Street, if you're so smart why don't you do such and such." Talk like that.

Even so, regular carpenter wasn't a bad job: outdoors, talking with Cabral and the other developers there on site. Then Lenny made me finish man. That was when the trouble really started. As finish man you come in contact with a lot of the owners, who usually don't know a joist from a tennis racket. Like I'm putting formica on a counter, and the guy says, "I thought it *came* that way!" Like formica grew on trees!

But when I say "owners," it's not just guys — women, too! I don't claim to be Mr. America, but I've had more than my share of interest from the opposite sex. Not just Donna and Rita and the girls down at Charlie's, either. I'm talking your professional women, your lawyers, engineers, doctors even.

You see their husbands in their designer sweats and running shoes, trying to start a power mower — you don't wonder these women are looking around. I don't claim to be a hunk, but a woman looks at me, she knows she's dealing with the masculine gender.

The main thing is, I guess I understand women, have a certain rapport with them. So it was never any big surprise, some of these women making a move on me. Happens all the time.

Last week took the prize. Lenny gave me my job Monday afternoon. New condo over in Cedar Farm. The lady asked for mahogany doors in the front entranceway, got the maple instead. Lenny said just take two new doors over, and the burnished hardware to go with them. "Number 14," he said. "Mrs. Sellers. She'll be there to let you in, but leaves for work at eight."

Well, I knew right then what *that* game was all about. Mrs. Sellers wasn't *Mrs.* Anything. She happened to be Rebecca Sellers I sat next to in homeroom senior year, eleven years ago. She went off to college somewhere. Now she's back. She was popular in high school, but never married, as far as I know.

So now she's pushing thirty, still single, and it's like I know it's tough for her. Hey, no joke, read *Time* magazine: a girl gets to be thirty, and her chances for finding a guy are zilch. Rebecca's no exception. I'll give you five to one: when she called about the maple doors, she knew I was Lenny's finish man. You know, among the girls, word gets around. They talk at aerobics class, the grocery store.

True, I didn't ask her to go out in high school. But she saw me every day in homeroom, got to know me. Maybe when she heard I was working right there, she got to thinking about me. Actually, I thought the thing with the doors was a fairly cool way to work it without attracting attention.

So I made it up to take the doors home in my van Monday night. That way I could get over there a little early the next morning, see what Rebecca Sellers was up to these days.

I rolled in her driveway at 7:25, time for a cup of coffee, sweet roll, whatever she wanted. This was her game plan, not mine. *She* complained about the maple doors, not me.

"Come on in," she called out when I rang the bell. "Mr. Ribeiro said you'd be here."

I heard the dishwasher start, heard her high heels click into the downstairs bathroom. Few minutes later she clicked right on out to the entranceway, where I was starting to take down doors.

One thing about Rebecca: she was always a good dresser. Grey suit, white satin blouse — she looked very professional, hair curled just enough to show there was a woman under there.

She didn't look at me. "Good," she said, touching the mahogany doors where I'd leaned them against the wall. "Thanks for getting here early." Then she bent over to pick up her brief case. "Will you just pull the door shut when you leave?"

I figured, whatever she planned, whatever she got all dolled up for: she couldn't pull it off. Maybe seeing me brought back too much for her, from senior year. Maybe she was somewhat embarrassed: her age, not having a regular guy. Maybe she just lost her courage. Hey, I can understand that.

Anyway, I decided to break the ice, help her out. I stopped with the doors, said her name. "Rebecca?"

She squinted, pretended to recognize me for the first time. "Robert?" she said, and "My God! Durfee High School!" She even remembered the name of the home room teacher. "I didn't recognize you," she said. "It must have been your hat." She glanced at my midsection. I admit, in eleven years, I've filled out somewhat. Hey, I got nothing to hide: I'm no high school kid.

"So you're teaching now?" I asked. I figured her for a teacher; she was always smart.

"Actually, I'm an account rep," she said. "Merrill Lynch."

Of course that got my interest. I told her investments were right down my alley, told her about a few of the projects I'd helped Cabral scope out. "There's a couple I'm not free to discuss," I said. I told her I was also interested in stocks and bonds, stuff like that. I said I wanted to take some time discussing it with her, but I had to get working on the doors. Anyway, she had her briefcase, ready to go. But I let her know I had a few specific investments I was looking at, might give her a call sometime. She nodded, interested, like she knew what I was getting at.

"Maybe we could have dinner sometime?" I said. I tried to think where I could take her. Hey! You don't want to take a girl like Rebecca to *Charlie's!*

Well, at that point in time her expression changed, like a light went on. All of a sudden it was a different story.

No, she said, thanks, but she didn't think so. No, she said, when I asked, it wasn't another guy. She hesitated for a second, held her breath, bit her lip, looked away, like she was ten years old, not 30, trying to think up an excuse, or maybe even reconsidering. Then she let out her breath, looked at me. "Robert," she said, "thanks for asking. Really."

"No problem," I told her. I thought, Hey! It wasn't *me* started it. It's not *my* chances turning to zilch. Not that it bothered me, it just makes you wonder. You try to be nice: is this what it gets you?

It surprised hell out of me when she reached to shake my hand, so I ended up dropping my screwdriver, giving her a wimp handshake.

"Great seeing you, Robert," she said. And there I was, half kneeling on the floor, her standing there in her fancy suit, holding me by the ends of my fingers. Jesus, I *hate* when somebody shakes hands like that!

* * * *

Next morning Lenny wanted to see me in his office in the trailer. He was pretty steamed. Apparently she'd called him at 11:30 the night before, woke him up. She got home a little before ten herself, fooled with the key and the lock and so on for an hour before the guy from the next unit came out to help her. Mr. Designer Sweats himself! Can't put up a cup hook without reading the directions. I'm surprised *he* figured it out, found her door was nailed shut.

Why would I do such a dumb stunt, Lenny wanted to know? Why couldn't I just do my job? I never saw Lenny so mad — and after nine years!

I let him know I was leaving anyway. I told him being finish man was a waste of my time. People didn't know what they wanted, I told him. I said if he'd utilized me to do some of his planning, listened to some of my business ideas, he wouldn't be wasting his time with all these two-bit jobs.

I don't know what hit me, but saying all this to Lenny, I got emotional. First my voice cracked, then my eyes filled up. This had never happened before. I thought: am I losing it? I just wanted to get out of there, not break down in front of Lenny.

It wasn't just the job. It was more like my whole life was hanging out there to see. *Why would I do such a dumb stunt?* If only I had the answer.

In the middle of it Bernadette, Lenny's bookkeeper, walked in. By now I was really crying. I couldn't go outside like that. I didn't know *where* to go, so I just sat down in a chair in the middle of the trailer, tried to wipe my face off, tried to stop, Lenny and Bernadette not saying a word.

Finally Bernadette said she's going over to the Donut Shop for coffee, would I like a donut or something? And this got me started again.

Lenny just kept his head down, pretending to shuffle papers. Another minute and he got up to leave. Had to get to work, he said, and would I just pull the door shut, and not lock it. Then he must have realized. "No shit, Bobby!" he said, "Bernadette didn't take her coat."

* * * *

Right now I'm not doing anything about a new job, but there's plenty of work out there. Especially for a guy with my experience. The only thing is: no more finish work. I'm totally burnt out on that. I want to get back outside, get some fresh air for a change. Or maybe something with Cabral, something in the planning area, that sort of thing. Otherwise, I'll sign up with a builder needs a regular carpenter.

Face it: I don't know what I'm going to do. Maybe I'll swing down to the Big Apple for a couple of days. I've still got over $300 left on my one Master Card. I'll check out Wall Street, take in a play, have a couple of good meals, drinks, the works.

Maybe Donna or Rita or one of the girls from Charlie's would like to tag along. We might even go to Madison Square Garden, see a hockey game! Isn't that perfect? Bruins fans — in *Madison Square Garden!* Hey! What I've been through, I could use a good laugh.

How Do You Know?

What if you hear something? What if you hear a child crying? Is it playing? Is it hurt? Is it afraid? Is it in trouble? How do you know?

Suppose there is a street, and houses, and driveways. The yards are wide. There are brick houses. The bricks are like red, except darker. The porches have screens and swings, and there are shadows, but there is white around the edge. There are trees. Some trees are called oak trees. And maple trees. Oak trees have acorns, which are something like nuts, and leaves with fingers. Maple trees have different leaves, not fingers — what do you call them? You shouldn't eat the acorns.

Sun is high up in the trees. Sun is on the roofs and the driveways. Sun stops at the end of the driveway. Then the street is almost dark, except where they took a tree away. They cut the tree up and a truck took it away. Sun comes through where they took the tree away.

People cut the grass and sweep. You have to sweep. The job isn't finished until you sweep. Some houses have white or purple flowers around the front steps. You call them irises. Some have pink and blue flowers. What are they called? Something. In one yard a lady stuck bricks in the ground, around the flowers. The bricks are like red, except darker. In one driveway the man parked his camper. Some houses have fans in the windows. The curtains move. The curtains move, but the trees are very quiet.

On one house there is a ramp. The ramp goes from the front porch to a landing, then to the sidewalk.

Anyway, what if it is before lunch? You are doing the back sidewalk. Mostly it is quiet, except for a child on a tricycle. The tricycle has a bell on it. Mostly it is quiet, but sometimes you hear the bell.

Then you hear a car come up the street. The car stops. Maybe the car stops and parks along the street. Maybe the car stops *in* the street. Maybe the driver looks for a number. Maybe the car pulls into a driveway and stops. Maybe it is a neighbor's car. After the car stops, mostly it is quiet again.

Then what if you hear something? What if you hear a child crying? Is it playing? Is it hurt? Is it afraid? Is it in trouble? How do you know? Are other children playing? Is the child alone? The child is not yours. Maybe you don't know the family. Maybe the child is only playing.

What if the child is crying again? Is it playing? Is it hurt? Is it afraid? Is it in trouble? How do you know? On television they tell children to cry. Make noise and cry, so someone will come and help.

Some children cry when they play. If the child is in trouble, it will go to its mother. The mother will know. Maybe the lady who stuck the bricks in the ground will know. Maybe no child is in trouble. Maybe the child is only playing.

* * * *

What if you live on the street, in the house with the ramp? You live in the house with the ramp, and your friends live there, and the house mother lives there. You and your friends live there, and each morning except Saturday and Sunday you and your friends go on the bus to the workshop. At the workshop you and your friends fold yellow price sheets, and put them in envelopes, and put the stamps on straight.

Each morning you and your friends go on the bus to the workshop, except Saturday and Sunday. On Friday you get paid, and on Saturday you walk to the drug store. It is only two blocks to the drug store, one traffic light. Look both ways. Sometimes the white police car is there. If the policeman says to go, you can go.

On Saturday you walk to the drug store and buy a candy bar. What is it called? It starts with a B. At the drug store you eat the candy bar, and look at magazines. Sometimes you buy a magazine with your money from the workshop. There is a magazine with cars. Once you bought the magazine with the swimming suit girls. You didn't show the swimming suit girls to the house mother.

Each morning you and your friends go on the bus to the workshop, except Saturday and Sunday. In the summer, Wednesday is different. On Wednesday in the summer you stay back and cut the grass at the house. It is your job to cut the grass and sweep. You don't like to sweep, but the job isn't finished until you sweep. Sweeping makes it look nice. The house mother tells you if you make the grass look nice she will get bricks to stick in the ground along the sidewalk. This is called a border.

What if you live in the house with the ramp, and it is Wednesday, and it is your job to cut the grass? It is before lunch. The sun is hot. There isn't any grape drink: that's only at night. You don't like to sweep, and you are edging the walk by the back porch. You think about your magazines, or about the bricks to make a border along the sidewalk.

Then a child is crying. You hear it crying, and you are edging the walk by the back porch. You hear it crying, and you are edging the walk and thinking about the bricks to stick in the ground to make a border along the sidewalk. You hear it crying, and the bell on the tricycle has stopped, and you remember being afraid. You hear the child crying, and you remember being afraid, and you go out front, and the child is across the street, and there is the car, and the car door is open, and there is a man in the car. Suppose the child is crying, and you go to her. What if you are the only one to go to her?

What if you go, and you see her holding on to the tricycle, and crying, and you see the car, and the man, and the car door is open, and you are the only one? You see her, afraid of the car, and you remember being afraid, and you go up to her and put your arm around her. What if you put your arm around her and the man sees you, and when he sees you he drives away, and you are the only one? She is still afraid of the car. She is still crying. You are the only one, and you put your arm around her. You remember being afraid, and you hold your arm around her until she stops crying.

What if her mother comes? What if the child's mother comes, finally, holding a towel around her head, and you want to tell the mother? But what if the mother screams, and then the child is crying again?

* * * *

Suppose there is a street, and houses. The mother holds her child. The child is crying. Other mothers come into the street. Grandmothers come into the street. Everybody is talking. Grandmothers come into the street and talk to the mother.

You live in the house with the ramp, and one of your friends comes out on the porch, and your house mother comes into the street, and puts her hand on your arm. The white police car rolls up the street and stops, and the door opens.

* * * *

What if you hear something? What if you hear a child crying? Is it playing? Is it hurt? Is it afraid? Is it in trouble? How do you know?

The Business with the Garbage

No one knew what she did for a living. Several times a week she emerged from her house in high heels, designer suits, stylish hats, hair and makeup just right, and drove out of the neighborhood in an almost-new Buick. But several times a week didn't seem like a regular job, and she was too young to be retired.

A few years back she bought number 13 at the head of the street, a large cape — too large, actually, for one person.

O'Brien's wife claimed to have seen her on TV, advertising plastic wrap. Someone said she was the previous governor's ex-girlfriend. Hart said ridiculous, that she was just a schoolteacher, probably a substitute.

Women sized up her rings, said she was divorced. But Baker's wife heard she was married once to a naval aviator shot down and killed in the first Gulf war. She didn't seem to have children, though at her age they could have been grown, living elsewhere. Feldman said she was pushing fifty, but people who got close enough saw only the faint hint of a wrinkle by each eye. Closer to forty, they guessed.

Mostly she kept to herself. She wasn't the sort of person any of the women in the neighborhood felt close to. First off, she was very attractive — striking, people said — and she dressed like a page out of *Vogue*. For example, her hats. Women did not wear hats like she wore — wide, stylish brims concealing half her face, and in every color imaginable.

Second, the southern accent, the aristocratic southern belle demeanor. The one woman who ever saw her kitchen (the excuse was to borrow an egg) said everything was copper, sterling, or fine china — even the everyday things. It was just a bit much, they said. True, she was stylish, had good manners, impeccable taste. But something wasn't quite right. What was it? "Let's just say she doesn't fit in," said one neighbor.

Not that the neighbors didn't try. They held a cookout to welcome her. She showed up carrying a crystal dish with some sort of vegetarian dip, back before vegetarian was chic. No one touched it. And of course she wore a hat to the cookout: a huge-brimmed sort of garden hat, red to match her dress. It bounced when she walked, waved when the breeze stirred.

"Don't you look nice!" they said. But they snickered among themselves. That's when they named her "The Hat Lady."

At first she got along with the men, until they heard the exchange she had with Hart, their financial guru, their tax and investment expert. At that first cookout, he tried to explain how soybean futures were traded. The Hat Lady listened quietly, sipping a vodka gimlet. When Hart got confused, she picked up the ball, finished the explanation. The men were impressed. Hart looked around, exasperated. "That's what I was getting to," he said. After that, men steered clear of her.

The neighbors invited her two or three times more, with the same results. She would make an early appearance in her stylish costume — always a dress and a hat. Neighbors greeted her politely, talked about parking space at the beach or the price of California lettuce. She had less to say; whatever she said drew skeptical remarks, at best, if not jokes and snickering. "Ballet?" said Feldman. "I wonder about some of those guys. I know I wouldn't go on stage dressed like that!" They waited for her to leave, so the party could go on. After she left, Baker imitated her southern accent in a falsetto drawl.

Eventually they no longer invited her. She seemed not to mind. She keeps to herself anyway, they said. But a neighborhood pattern was disturbed. Neighbors didn't discuss it, but had you asked, they might have blamed her independence. When someone new moved in, usually they needed help: they borrowed your phone, asked about appliance dealers, church schedules, asked the neighborhood daughters to baby sit. Not the Hat Lady: she had everything arranged in advance, phones installed, washer and dryer hooked up. She didn't need baby sitters. In a way, it was like she didn't need neighbors, didn't need the neighborhood. What kind of new neighbor is that?

On her side: she was generous to kids selling raffle tickets and Girl Scout cookies. Paper boys and girls got good tips. But the older kids seemed to sense she didn't really belong there.

At Halloween her house got more attention than others. The first year she left her car in the driveway on Cabbage Night, and the windows were soaped all around. The face of a witch with missing teeth was soaped on the back window, a misspelled obscenity on the side. After that she parked in her garage. Still there would be an egg splattered on her garage door, a trash can upended on the front sidewalk.

One Christmas O'Brien's oldest, on vacation from Boston College, had a party. One of his fraternity brothers misjudged a U-turn at the end of the street, leaving an eight-inch rut in the Hat Lady's yard. Neither O'Brien nor his son said anything to her about it, and the next day when her yard man showed up to shovel snow, he made repairs to the lawn as well. When a baseball went through her side window one summer, the same kids who got Little League contributions from her in the spring ran from the scene. No one admitted responsibility; parents ignored it.

People moving in understood her to be the neighborhood recluse, didn't ask for an explanation. For many, the hats were explanation enough. She continued to come and go in exotic, colorful creations.

One Sunday morning her old cat lay in the street in front of her house, its head run over. Everyone guessed Baker's son had done it. But Baker acted like nothing happened. No one came forward to make amends, express regrets. This time the Hat Lady did not wait for her yard man. Wearing leather boots and long black gloves, she used a pick and shovel to excavate a grave in her back yard, laid the animal to rest.

Considering the ups and downs over the years, most neighbors were surprised she got involved in the garbage strike. Actually it was after the strike, the first day they collected after returning.

The strike itself was the end result of the EPA ruling. The town increased user fees at the landfill. Medeiros, the contractor handling residential garbage, was quick to react. He jacked up the rates for garbage collection, laid off half his men, increased the size of the routes, left the remaining workers to make up the difference.

That triggered the strike, a disorganized sort of thing. A union organizer came in from Brockton, claimed to represent the collectors. But one of the drivers showed up on TV, claimed to be in charge of the strike. Reporters were confused. TV coverage flagged. The collectors themselves seemed confused, and after not collecting for two weeks they returned to their jobs without fanfare.

The strike was a temporary nuisance, but mostly neighbors joked about it, the lack of organization, the conflicting claims of leadership. Some of the collectors were young Portuguese men, and in the neighborhood ethnic jokes abounded, especially when Rodrigues was around to take the brunt of them. Rodrigues gave back in kind: if his father hadn't supported the Irish on welfare, he said, O'Brien would be collecting garbage himself, and so on.

When the garbage truck rolled into the neighborhood the first week after the strike, the street was lined not only with the usual garbage cans, but overflowing boxes and containers of every size and description, accumulated during the three weeks. Several neighbors stood in their driveways waiting for the truck, wanting to be sure the extra things were picked up.

The Hat Lady's driveway was the first stop, and the truck lingered there at the top of the street. One of the men appeared to be drinking a cup of coffee beside the truck, another had gone inside the yard, also drinking out of a white Styrofoam cup. The truck's engine growled idly, but nothing happened.

Finally, after waiting a few minutes in his driveway, Feldman waddled up the street impatiently, arms extended, holding a white plastic garbage bag in each hand. He said something to the man standing by the truck at the end of the Hat Lady's driveway, drinking his coffee. The man, a lanky black man nearly a foot taller than Feldman, took both bags in one hand, smiled at him smoothly, and with a flick of his wrist tossed them into the truck through the opening in the side. Feldman pointed back down the street at the three-week accumulation of trash and garbage stacked along the street, said something else to the man. But by then the man was back to his coffee. The driver, just inside the Hat Lady's yard, leaned on the fence post. The Hat Lady was barely visible behind the louvered storm door in the walkway between her house and garage. After a few more minutes, the men finished their coffee, threw the cups into the truck, continued down the street.

Talking among themselves, people blamed the Hat Lady. By giving the men coffee, she seemed to be supporting the strike, at least supporting the collectors. Certainly it wasn't showing solidarity with the neighbors. At best, it delayed the collection.

Later, one of the neighbors said Feldman insulted the man. Hardly, said Feldman. "All I said was, people are waiting to carry those cans back when you boys finish."

That morning, in the house next door to Feldman's, one of the plastic bags broke, spilling potato peels and bread wrappers onto the edge of Feldman's front yard.

There were phone calls to Medeiros. Feldman would not admit he called. But the next week the coffee break at the Hat Lady's was longer. Afterward the men swept down the street in a fury, scattering cans and lids, making up time. Several neighbors reported cans were untouched. When they called Medeiros, a receptionist reminded them there was a limit of two cans.

Baker was furious. For years the collectors had taken whatever was set out. "The prices we're paying, and they're blowing the whistle on us for too many cans?" He bought a new four-wheel drive, canceled garbage collection service with an angry letter to Medeiros. Each Saturday from then on he drove out of the neighborhood with his own trash.

He urged others to haul their own garbage to the dump. But the idea never caught on. Too many people had no way to transport cans. Some of the elderly could hardly drag them out to the curb, much less lift them in and out of cars. Instead, people became more careful about fitting their garbage into the prescribed two cans, seeing it was wrapped in the specified way.

Meanwhile the coffee breaks at the Hat Lady's continued, got even longer. Now she appeared in the yard in a colored turban, refilling the men's cups. But the neighbors looked the other way. After enduring the strike, witnessing the confrontation between Feldman and the collector, listening to Baker's angry words, most were happy to have the trash collected at all, were willing to chase down their cans and lids once a week, sweep up the spills, whatever was required to get the neighborhood back to normal.

But then Wednesday before Thanksgiving, the Christmas letter showed up in people's mail boxes. The letter was done in a decorative computer font; neatly, with correct spelling and grammar; reproduced on pink paper. It talked about the people who keep the community running: nurses and doctors, policemen, firemen, teachers — and trash collectors. It talked about the teachers' union, the firemen's strike of two years back. It talked about doctors' yachts and condominiums, their fees. It listed average salaries of "the various professions" — "Trash collector" at the bottom. The letter recalled the two-week strike, how difficult it was without trash collectors. *Isn't it ironic,* the letter wanted to know, *a service so necessary, with such small rewards? But you can make a difference,* it reassured the neighbors.

You can make a difference, it said, *at this season when we strive to right wrongs, to correct injustices.*

On the reverse was a "suggested giving schedule." It listed household income brackets, suggested gifts for the trash collectors. Senior citizens, on fixed incomes, were given special consideration, but it was still a hefty sum. There was even a form to fill out. December 8 was listed as the "Giving Date." Or — above a certain amount — the gift could be spread out over three weeks. *Would you eat at a restaurant,* the letter asked, *without leaving a tip?*

The neighborhood buzzed. People talked to one another in pairs, inside their kitchens, or in the TV rooms at night. Smith called it blackmail, declared openly he would have nothing to do with it. Hart estimated collectors would get a few hundred dollars each. "Ridiculous," he said.

Several of the neighbors did not want to talk about the letter. Even some who complained were indefinite about their giving plans for the trash collectors. A couple of the wives reported arguing with their husbands over what to do, what to give. At one Thanksgiving gathering, a wife said maybe it was good these guys had jobs, weren't on welfare. Maybe it was costing taxpayers less in the long run. There was an embarrassed silence until one of the husbands changed the subject, switched on the pregame show.

No one wanted to talk about who wrote the letter. Of course no one spoke to the Hat Lady about it.

A few people tried calling Medeiros. They either got the answering service, or the sassy receptionist. "It's up to you," she told them, "you and the collector. We don't have anything to do with Christmas gifts." No, she said, there wasn't any letter sent out. She didn't know anything about a letter, she said.

On December 8, the "Giving Date," most of the garbage cans in the neighborhood had white envelopes taped to the lids. On a few, the envelope was decorated with a stick-on red or green ribbon. The coffee break was shorter that morning. The men proceeded down the street more deliberately. They removed the envelopes carefully, passed them to the driver. The driver made a notation on each envelope, collected them in a cardboard portfolio. In front of one elderly woman's house, one of the collectors removed a small package wrapped in foil and red ribbon from the lid of the can. He handed the attached envelope to the driver, tore off the foil and red ribbon wrapping. It was a small cake. He ate it on the spot, tossed the crumbs and wrapping into the back of the truck.

The following week the coffee break was longer, and on December 22 the men didn't have their coffee outside but disappeared through the louvered doors, evidently into the Hat Lady's kitchen.

The collection that day was a little messier than usual. Some said it was because the men emerged none too steady from the Hat Lady's kitchen after their coffee. A lot of neighbors seemed uncomfortable talking about it.

On Christmas morning all the lights in Baker's outdoor tree were missing, but no one paid any attention to this: kids stole lights every year. Baker replaced them before most people noticed, didn't talk about it with anyone.

It was the second or third week in January, Hart had words with Johnson, his next-door neighbor. Before it was over they both got pretty vocal. People said Hart accused Johnson of caving in to the garbage collectors. "Every week," Hart said, "my yard is a disaster area. Meanwhile you're over here fat, dumb, and happy." Johnson said Hart's yard was a disaster area *before* the garbage collectors came, and if he would spend a little time cleaning up, instead of worrying about what wasn't his business, it would help the whole neighborhood. And so on like that.

People noticed whose garbage was collected neatly, whose was tossed around, left in the cans, etc. People took sides, made accusations. One neighbor told another her kid was disloyal for offering to clean up yards and driveways after the weekly collections.

The few who still called Medeiros got the answering service, or got put on hold by the sassy receptionist. If she finally got back to them, she'd insist they had to give complaints to Medeiros himself, she could only take a message. "You should check what size bags you're using," she told them. "Are you using the cheap bags? We got to have regulations too, you know."

Baker openly ridiculed his neighbors, said the neighborhood could have avoided the trouble had everybody followed his lead, hauled their own trash. Then one morning both the rear tires on Baker's four-wheel drive were flat. Baker was incensed, immediately claimed it was vandalism. But O'Brien pointed out the roofing nails in each tire. "That looks like something you picked up at the dump," he said.

A few times on Wednesdays, after the routes were finished, the garbage truck returned to the neighborhood, parked in front of the Hat Lady's. A couple of the houses in the neighborhood went up for sale.

Feldman, however, wasn't ready to give in yet. He bought a bright new four-wheel drive, showed it off to Baker amid much bravado and backslapping in the driveway. But the second time he hauled his garbage Feldman had a stroke right there at the dump. By the time the emergency squad arrived, he had lost the use of his right side, couldn't utter a coherent sound. He went from the hospital into a nursing home. His wife moved in with her sister. His nephew drove away the four-wheel drive after the moving van left. Feldman's house was the fifth in the neighborhood to go up for sale.

By July *several* trucks stopped for coffee in the morning. Not only on Wednesdays, but Mondays and Fridays, they rolled in and out of the neighborhood.

Neighbors talked about what to do, but most were at a loss. Rodrigues, next door to the Hat Lady, complained about trucks parked in front of his house, blocking his driveway. No one could reach the company. Calls to the town hall never seemed to find the right official in his office. The Council was in recess for summer vacation.

Smith played golf with the chief of police, talked to him about the coffee break situation, about the other trucks' stopping.

"You're not telling me they're disorderly?" the chief said. "They just drink coffee?" He eyed Smith skeptically. "Seems to me they're within their rights," he said. The other two in the foursome said Medeiros collected in their neighborhoods, but they knew nothing of these coffee breaks. "What Christmas letter?" they asked.

Smith's house was up for sale the next week. O'Brien and Rodrigues laughed at him, said he was overreacting. Privately, they too were worried. Several more *For Sale* signs went up.

Within a month it seemed a third of the neighborhood was up for sale. People made excuses for leaving. They pointed out property values had been up sharply the last ten years, and many of them were sitting on large capital gains. They talked about the money they could get selling their homes, the new camper they could buy, the vacations, Caribbean cruises. "Now might be a good time," they said. They said it had nothing to do with the business with the garbage.

Houses for sale in the neighborhood sat empty for months. Buyers from other parts of town knew of the garbage collectors' Christmas gift in this neighborhood. But the problem wasn't money. It was the letter, the trouble surrounding the gifts, the fact only this one neighborhood was affected. The business with the garbage had taken on a life of its own. The neighbors all knew it; privately, they worried. Property values would go to hell, they said. "It's worse than that," said O'Brien's wife. "We'll *all* go to hell."

By now most had given in, tried to convince the rest to do the same. As the following Thanksgiving approached, only Hart and Baker held out.

In early November Hart tried to organize a campaign against the Christmas gifts. But a week later he was hit with an IRS audit. For years, apparently, he'd called himself a church, for tax purposes, and was deducting his household expenses accordingly.

The following week Baker had a contractor sink posts in concrete at the corners of his yard, along the edges. He put a chain link fence around both his front and back yards, put a padlock on the gate at the end of his front walk, got a German shepherd to patrol the perimeter. Baker used to take a vacation with his wife, just after Labor Day, but that fall they stayed home. The only time anyone saw him outside was on Saturdays, raking leaves. When the trees were bare, he watched television all day.

The Christmas gift letter came out again during Thanksgiving week. This time most neighbors didn't talk about it at all. It was given to everyone in the neighborhood, Medeiros customers or not. It chided former customers for breaking off their service. *Not pulling together,* the letter called it. *Let's restore pride to our community,* it said. This year people were tight-lipped.

Saturday night after Thanksgiving neighbors were settled down before their TV's. The neighborhood was quiet, a slight breeze stirring through the bare trees. The nine o'clock movie started. Just as the movie maker's logo filled the screen, before the music came up, there was a shot. A few of the neighbors thought it was part of the movie, a trick to get attention. But outside dogs were barking, and a second shot interrupted the opening bars of the movie theme.

Outside, Baker's security floodlights were on. Up and down the street porch lights came on, doors opened. Baker was on his front walk, holding a shotgun, just fired. He seemed drunk, mumbled somebody had been tampering with his car. When people looked they saw the side window of his four-by-four blasted out clean. Apparently he had blown out the window of his own car. By then a police cruiser was on the scene, turning the fronts of the houses alternately blue and red. Neighbors gathered around Baker's fence. The officers shined their lights around, mostly to get house numbers for their report. No one, not even Baker, could say for sure they saw anyone even *in* the neighborhood, much less tampering with anybody's car.

Eventually the police turned off their lights and left. The crowd disappeared, leaving Baker's four-by-four there in the glare of the security lights, the side window shot out, a puddle of shattered glass alongside.

Next morning the police were back. They appeared at Baker's door apologetically, explained they had to book him for discharging a firearm in a residential neighborhood. Baker wouldn't go with them, and one of the officers returned to the car, used the radio. After a while the chief arrived in another cruiser, talked to Baker for 15 minutes, and eventually both cars left, Baker riding with the chief. Baker agreed to plead disturbing the peace, paid a small fine plus court costs.

After that he stayed inside, rarely drove his car. His wife said he stopped eating, couldn't remember things. His son came by for a few months, took care of the house, hauled the trash. By now Baker couldn't get dressed or go to the bathroom by himself. Hart visited once or twice, but the best he could do was advise that Baker should be in a nursing home. Hart drove the car the day they took him.

* * * *

Not many of the old neighbors live there anymore. There's O'Brien, but actually it's his son's house now. O'Brien himself lives mostly in one room upstairs, has his own TV, keeps his shades down most of the time. He had a small stroke a year or so back, and there was talk of putting him in a nursing home, but nothing's been done about that. Not until the sewer job is finished. Apparently the original sewer connection to the street collapsed, and for a month none of O'Brien's toilets would flush. The front yard is still dug up from installing the new line, and young O'Brien needs his father's social security to pay the contractor to finish that job.

Rodrigues still lives at number 11, but he's renting the house from the bank: he no longer owns it. He was buying up all the houses he could at the height of the garbage scare, got himself too highly leveraged, then lost it when the market turned down.

Nobody's heard much from Baker or Feldman since they went to the nursing home. A month after Smith moved away his wife divorced him to marry the spring water delivery man.

Hart had a condominium in Aruba (a "branch" of his so-called church) and for a while spent most of his time there. The house stood vacant much of the year. The IRS held a lien on both homes, while Hart appealed the church deduction issue. Eventually he settled with the IRS, gave them *both* houses, now lives with a daughter in Fall River.

And of course there's the Hat Lady, still living in number 13, at the head of the street. She gets out quite a bit, eats out most nights, still looks marvelous. Striking, the new neighbors call her. They find her congenial. A few even call her their friend.

If anyone asks her about the business with the garbage, she shrugs. "I never understood all the fuss," she says. "Myself, I never had a problem."

"After all," she says, quoting the most recent letter, "trash collection makes the neighborhood a nicer place to live."

Honest Work

At my last checkup my blood pressure had been up again. The doc got on me about that, and my weight.

"Are you getting any exercise?" he wanted to know.

"Some," I lied. I haven't played racquetball for four years. Can't remember the last time I rode a bike or ran.

He also gave me his speech about stress, about not taking things too seriously, about smelling the flowers, and so on. I wanted to ask him what I should do about my quarterly sales quotas while I smell all these flowers.

Anyway, to get him off my back, I got serious. Lost five pounds, pretty much held to three or four cups of coffee a day, except for a week I was in San Francisco for the sales meeting. Then when the weather got better, I walked the three miles to work.

In fact I was walking the day I ran into the guy in the mall. I never saw him before that day, but from a distance he was a picture from my high school literature book — flowing white beard, long wavy white hair. From the neck up he was Henry Wadsworth Longfellow. We were the only two people on foot in that empty section of the parking area of the mall. He seemed to be approaching me.

He was forty, at most, not only broader and heavier but several inches taller than me. He was wearing washed-out brown work fatigues. His hair and beard had grown together into a dingy grey shrub, tinted with yellow tobacco stains.

As we got closer he put up a hand. "Can you give me a push?" he asked. I said I was sorry, I didn't have my car. He acted almost offended. "Not with your car," he said. "Last time anybody pushed me with their car it scratched the hell out of my paint job." He seemed to be sizing me up, seeing if I was fit for the task.

Walking to and from the office I wore running shoes, left a pair of regular shoes at work and changed when I got there in the morning. I had on a blue nylon knapsack, carrying home work to do that night. Otherwise I was dressed for the office.

He grinned at my running shoes. "You look like you need the exercise," he said.

Frankly, I didn't appreciate the guy's attitude, but in sales you learn to handle all types. "Okay," I said, trying to go along with his joke. "You're going to put me to work."

"Nobody needs to tell me what work is," he said, turning to lead the way. "I never knew anybody that died of honest work."

That gratuitous little speech caught me by surprise, but I figured he was stressed out about the car. I kept my mouth shut and followed a step behind. His arms and hands were huge, the seat of his pants stained with grease.

As we started across the lot I saw his car stopped near the entrance, only fifty yards from the Sears Garage. I wondered what this repair bill would set him back. I imagined him paying it off at fifteen dollars a month, god knows what percent interest.

Every six months when I took my leased car for service I paid with the company credit card. I ordered a new car every two years. Except for occasionally tweaking the electronics it never needed repairs.

Longfellow pointed to a phone booth at the side entrance of Food Fair. "You got any change?" he asked. "I need to call my old lady." I found a couple of quarters in my pocket and gave them to him. By this time I wasn't anxious to lend him my cell phone.

He veered off toward the phone booth. I stayed in the center of the parking lot while he phoned. The walking put a tingle of circulation in my ankles and feet. After only two weeks of that, I already felt better. Maybe I could get somebody at work to play some racquetball again.

Longfellow filled the narrow booth, holding the phone to his ear with his left hand, gesturing with his right. Soon he hung up, but remained in the booth. He turned away from the open door to light a cigarette, then put the second quarter in the phone, made another call. He was talking and gesturing again.

I saw I wouldn't be home by six to catch the news. But I remembered about smelling the flowers. Forget the news, I thought. Relax.

The wind stirred, and I realized my wool suit coat didn't do much to keep me warm.

Longfellow finished his calls and stepped out again. He motioned to me to follow him.

As I caught up to him, he seemed preoccupied with the phone calls. "Everything under control?" I asked, just making small talk.

"You bet it's under control," he said. "I see to it things are under control!" It was as if I had accused him of something. He kept walking, looked straight ahead, more like talking to himself than to me. "Enough craziness in the world as it is," he went on, "without letting your own affairs get out of control." It didn't make any sense, but I started feeling responsible, like I was responsible for the craziness in the world, like I had caused his car trouble.

Entering the shopping center, two cars crept past Longfellow's disabled car, the drivers looking at it sideways as they passed.

It was a monstrous old Cadillac, the kind of car they made back when gas was a dollar a gallon. The ads for that model compared it to a luxury liner. The original paint on Longfellow's car was either grey or faded blue. The right front fender was replaced but not repainted. It was maroon. Rust-retardant paint — a shade lighter than the maroon fender — spotted the bottom of the right passenger door.

The front bumper carried two expired security stickers from Lackland Air Force Base. A large red-on-white bumper sticker announced: GOD IS MY COPILOT. Another: FANTASY LAND — HORSE CAVE. In the back was a small boy, about four. The kid stood looking over the seat. His eyes followed his father. He'd been eating from a family-size bag of potato chips open on the front seat. Crumbs of potato chips ringed his mouth. One side of his face was smeared. It looked like he'd wiped crumbs off with his hand. When he saw his father returning he took another potato chip.

Longfellow went around to the driver's side and put his right arm through the window, shifting the car into neutral and taking hold of the steering wheel. The keys were still in the ignition. He took a last drag from his cigarette and flipped it away. He braced his left hand on the window frame, ready to push.

I realized it was a while since I'd pushed a car. I wanted to hold up my end of the bargain, was glad for the extra walking I'd been doing. I took my position on the passenger side, glanced at the Sears store. A folding door opened into a repair bay with stacks of tires all around.

"Straight for that side entrance?" I asked.

"No. To the gas station," Longfellow answered. He straightened up, looked at me over the top of the car. "Why would I want to go to Sears Roebuck?"

"That station is self-serve," I said. "Gas only. They can't do repairs." I filled up there all the time, passing my credit card to a teenage clerk inside the booth.

Longfellow seemed impatient to get started. "Repairs?" he said. "I don't need any repairs. I'm out of gas." He was matter of fact, like maybe *I* was slow to catch on.

The gas station was 300 yards across the mall, only seconds away in a car. But on foot, even for the two of us, pushing the car that far would be an effort. I asked if he couldn't just buy a gallon of gas and carry it to the car.

"I'm not about to give anybody $3.98 for a plastic can to carry a quart of gas in," he said. It sounded like he'd had a run-in with the kid in the station. "He wouldn't just let me use one," he said. "You've got to buy them."

I was having a hard time convincing myself I should push that monster 300 yards to save $3.98. I tried to persuade Longfellow the plastic container was a good buy. "It's probably not a bad thing to have in your trunk," I offered weakly. I even started to offer to buy it myself. "I've got the four bucks," I said.

But Longfellow wouldn't hear it. "I'm not looking for a handout," he said. He gestured with both hands in mock helplessness. "Look, if you don't think you can handle this, then okay. If you're so busy you can't take a minute to help me and my kid, fine."

Relax, I said to myself. The first principle of sales: The customer is always right. I decided to shut up and get it over with. "Okay," I said, bracing my hands against the window frame, ready to push. "It was just a suggestion."

Despite its size, the car started rolling easily. Partly because of the adrenalin I released into the first push. Actually, the effort felt good. Nice to see I could still cut it. I lifted some weights in college. Maybe after racquetball I could work out on one of those weight machines.

Longfellow steered around a pothole. He skirted the drain in the center of the lot, missing a stack of twigs, a Styrofoam cup, a battered carton left by the melted snow.

Even when I felt myself getting a little tired, I knew we had enough momentum to make it. I was mentally calculating the remaining distance to the gas station when I heard the right rear door open behind me. I looked around. The boy sat on the edge of the back seat, holding the door open, leaning over to watch the pavement move slowly by beneath the car.

I stopped to slam the door. The car stopped rolling, and Longfellow was quick to react. "We were going good," he said. "I wish you'd told me you were going to quit in the middle of it."

"I wish you'd told me he was going to open the door!" I shot back. By now I realized this guy wasn't out to win the good will award, but I couldn't let that one go by.

He almost laughed in my face. "One mile an hour?" he said. "What were you afraid would happen?"

Calm down, I told myself. "Look," I said. "I'm sorry. A moving car. The door open. It's just not my idea of safe. It's your kid I'm looking out for."

Longfellow braced his hands on the frame. "Why don't we just try to push," he said to me, "instead of arguing how to raise my kid?" Then he barked at the boy. "Ethan," he said, "leave those potato chips alone until you eat your supper."

I was out of breath, out of patience, but there was *no way* I would let this bastard get to me. I thought of Berger, the purchasing agent at Aetna, 2003. He made Longfellow look like a pussycat. Believe me, I've taken it from experts. Don't worry about it, I told myself. Just push the car.

There was still sand from the winter's snow treatment in that section of the parking lot. My feet slipped as I tried to start up again.

"You'd think those expensive sneakers would hold up better than that," said Longfellow. He was on solid ground on his side, although he couldn't move the car by himself.

"I'm in sand over here," I said.

"Don't I know about sand?" said Longfellow. He straightened up and wiped the back of his hand across his beard. "You know, I put up the parking garage down by Commercial Wharf. Now *that* was sand. You ever try using a front loader in sand to move around two-ton sections of steel?"

Even in the chilly wind I felt sweat on my forehead from the effort. My shirt was clammy against my shoulders from the knapsack straps. Using my feet, I scraped clear a space of pavement to stand on without slipping.

My left arm and shoulder were stiff. I flexed them and braced again for the push.

The car wouldn't move. I grunted with the effort. I heard nothing from Longfellow. How hard was he pushing? I wondered. Was he pushing at all? I braced again, put all my strength into it. It felt as if all the blood in my body went to the top of my skull. It was the first time I remembered feeling the very instant a headache started.

Finally it felt like I was slowly bending the frame of the car. I knew we were moving forward. No cars in the gas station. One car about to pull into the inside row of pumps.

I called out, "Steer for the outside pumps."

The only reply came from the kid. He fired an imaginary gun at me through the window. "Bam bam bam! Bam bam bam!" Plus every time the car hit a bump he made explosion sounds.

The huge Cadillac reached the concrete apron of the gas station, glided under the mercury vapor lamps just as they went on. The car rolled to a stop before it passed the pumps. The clerk in the toll booth was finishing a sandwich. My legs felt weak and unsteady, not completely under control. I held onto the frame of the car, waiting for the ground to feel solid under me.

Longfellow glanced at the clerk, then at me. I half expected he'd ask me to pay for the gas. Instead, he lit another cigarette, looked at the clock. "I didn't think it would take any 25 minutes just to get this car pushed into the gas station."

I wasn't feeling that great: dizzy, nauseous. I almost asked the clerk to call a cab. Instead I decided to rest a minute. Catch my breath. Took off the knapsack and dropped it. Sat down right there, on the curb.

The boy leaned out the window. Pointed his finger at my shoes. "Bam bam bam! Bam bam bam!" he said.

Last thing I remember, he made a huge explosion sound, leveling the gas station, the stores, the entire parking lot. With that everything went black.

* * * *

I came to when they lifted me. I was breathing from a mask over my face. "Take it easy," someone told me. "Relax. It's okay." As they fastened me in, I heard Longfellow outside. "I never saw him before in my life," he said. "He came out of nowhere, like to scared the Bejesus out of my kid." I could imagine him, gesturing with his cigarette. His tone went from excited to self-righteous. "You have to watch yourself out in these malls," he said. "Nowadays," he said, "you never know who you might run into."

The History of Psychiatric Nursing

Murphy's law: my first meeting with Doctor Woods, and I'm late. I'm supposed to be there now, and my hair isn't even brushed. Well, I can't help it. One of my patients was coming unglued. Girl's been here only a month, still having trouble settling in. Hearing what she's been through, it's no wonder. I'm sorry, but I can't just *leave* another woman like that. For me, that's what good nursing care is all about.

Then I had to take the back staircase getting up here. I can't stand that crowd hanging around the main lobby, that bitch at the reception desk. Of course with all the excitement I missed my cigarette break. Don't ever mention that around here. All you get is that crap about second-hand smoke.

Screw the cigarette. I don't want to get off on the wrong foot with Doctor Woods. She's the first woman shrink I've had in this department. I say, *High time!* Actually I expected her to be older, but no problem. We'll get along fine. The younger ones aren't as set in their ways, don't think they know everything before you even open your mouth.

Anyway, I'm giving Doctor Woods an article she might be interested in. I don't know what school of psychiatry she's involved in, but the article is by Modell, before he wrote his book. He gets into the idea of memory, how it's a reconstruction of what happened, not an exact record. So what is psychotherapy about? The patient's reconstruction of what happened, or the shrink's? Anyway, she might be interested. At least it can be an icebreaker. The main thing is, stick to the subject, don't skip around.

Also I'll tell her about the article I'm working on, about the history of psychiatric nursing. I'm sending it to the *Journal of Nursing*. A lot of people around here don't like it when I get started on this, but I can certainly tell her some history.

One story in particular might interest her. It's true, of course. I was one of eight women responsible for wings, or nursing units, in what was called "The Annex" — the women's side of the state general hospital. Doctor Woods is too young to remember, but believe me, the state general hospital was nothing like this. In those days it was more a warehouse than a hospital: no private rooms, just patients in these little nooks. Everything they owned was there — little porcelain animals, wooden plaques from the mountains or some beach in New Hampshire, cardboard containers of paper flowers, pictures of their families. Some of them with children kept their kids' pictures up to date.

In those days the sexes were strictly segregated: separate treatment, separate recreation, separate living arrangements. It was a tough job, a lot of responsibility. And I didn't pull rank on anyone: I worked hard, pitched in wherever I was needed. Of course I wasn't a nurse, I was an attendant. Actually, a sort of auxiliary attendant, but the way I did my job, it worked out to the same thing. In fact, I worked harder than any of the nurses, had as much or more responsibility for actual care. For example, if someone had to be restrained, or talked down, or something had to be cleaned up, I usually ended up doing it myself. And The Annex was no piece of cake. Some of those women were pretty tough, could hold their own in a fight, and did! Several of the other girls would rather have worked the men's side.

And they complained constantly. My friend Marie called it the salt mines. Personally, I just kept a professional attitude. My feeling was: that's what this hospital is for, people with problems. If nobody had any problems, they wouldn't need the hospital. Where would that have left me?

I always felt you could accomplish more by listening to these women than by restraining them. They would come to my room and talk. I lived right there at the hospital. I still took some medication. Big deal! Any time I wanted I could have moved out of there, got my own apartment. But why would I have done that? I was helping people there at the hospital, right? A lot of the other patients depended on those talks with me, depended on me to listen. I don't claim to be a shrink; sometimes you don't need a shrink, just someone to listen.

You heard all kinds of stories from those women: why they were there, what they did on the outside, what people did to them. What their families did to them. What their fathers did to them. It broke your heart.

There was a young redheaded girl from Connecticut. Her name was Gwendolyn. She was just over five feet, weighed practically nothing, her long red hair almost to her waist.

Her stepfather used her to entertain his drinking buddies, then complained about her not eating, criticized her because there wasn't any meat on her bones. Of course, wouldn't you know: *she* ended up in the hospital, while he was still out on the street, running loose. It made you wonder, How did the world get so screwed up? How did people get so screwed up? What *wouldn't* people do? Then again, the stories you heard, you never knew what was true and what wasn't.

Gwendolyn was one of the people I was able to help, at least for a while. She came to me at a particularly stressful time in her life. Well, I helped her as best I could. Let's say Gwendolyn died in captivity. Patients made token suicide attempts all the time. The hospital called them "suicide gestures." They tried to isolate the at-risk patients, keep them away from anything harmful. But Gwendolyn outsmarted them. She stocked up on pills, saved them. One night she just ate her whole supply, then went to bed. She didn't tell anybody, didn't leave a note. Nobody knew until the next morning.

Believe me, this sort of thing can only happen if there is a nursing screw-up. Either they weren't monitoring her medications, or she was getting them from someone else, or both. Plus, the night it happened they must have sloughed off on the bed checks. In any event, somebody should have been fired, but of course it got covered over. Nobody was at fault, it was unavoidable, and so on.

I wasn't responsible for her wing when it happened. If I *had* been, it never would have happened. *Nothing* is unavoidable if you give a damn, if you're at all professional.

But I'm getting away from the story. There was a small dental clinic there at the hospital. It was staffed two days a week: one day for male patients, the other for women from The Annex. I knew the dentist, in fact dated him for a while. He was older, but not that much: late thirties, maybe. He was small and slender, with dark, curly hair. He seemed even younger. His name was Szczepaniak, which of course no one could pronounce, so people called him Doctor Z. He was a really nice guy, not superior like a lot of doctors. I'll admit Doctor Z was sort of quiet, and took everything seriously. I didn't mind. Some guys can't stop talking about themselves. To others everything's a big joke.

Even when we were alone, I called him Doctor Z. I never referred to him or talked about him in a familiar way to the other girls. In fact, I wanted to keep it a secret. Fat chance! They all kidded me about him. Doctor Intense, they called him. I didn't care. Doctor Z *was* intense. That's what I liked about him. It made you feel things really mattered.

For one thing, his work really mattered. He was there at the hospital for the two clinic days, spent the rest of the week at other state hospitals. He threw himself into his work, put in long hours, took a real interest in the patients' welfare. If quitting time came, and there were still patients waiting, he kept going until everyone was taken care of. A nurse and a hygienist worked for him, but many nights he'd be there long after they went home. He took time with each patient, explained the treatment or the procedure, did it carefully. Sometimes at night he spent an hour or two with a single patient.

That meant our dates wouldn't start until ten or ten thirty, but that was okay. Usually by then we'd just stay around the hospital — my room, or the dental clinic. We could have gone anywhere we wanted, of course. He had money. I had money on account; all I had to do was ask for it. But I liked just being with him, listening to the things he said.

He told me about the plants in his office: five or six different varieties of fern, African violets, something he called a spider plant. Where I lived there were never flowers or plants. He knew the history of each plant, where it originated, the Latin name. He showed me how to identify each leaf. Really, he knew everything.

Yet at the same time he was simple and unaffected. In the clinic, with his white coat on, he was completely professional. But when we were alone, I could close my eyes, put my arms around him, and he could have been my high school sweetheart, home on leave from the Navy.

The whole time I was dating him I felt so much better, brilliant actually. And my meds were way down: some weeks I got by on two-fifty, three-hundred milligrams a day.

Sometimes, if he was a little tired, it was okay with me. Then we would just talk, or spend a quiet time together. I knew it was for the best, all the hard work he was doing, the long hours, the good he was accomplishing for the other patients. They took better care of their teeth, talked about cutting back on sweets. Their whole outlook got better. Gwendolyn, for one. She told me later Doctor Z was the first person at the hospital who treated her like a human being. No question he was making a difference, certainly with the women patients. And he wasn't a shrink, he was a *dentist!* It makes you wonder, doesn't it?

But you could never get him to talk about himself. What were his plans? Why wasn't he in private practice? Why had he worked for the state this long? Most doctors stayed with the state just long enough to complete their residency, or pay back a grant. Then they wanted to get established. But Doctor Z seemed to want something else. One night I asked him if he would set up his own practice someday.

He looked surprised, almost hurt. "This *is* my practice," he told me. I guess *I* looked surprised, or something. He always seemed to know what you were thinking. Anyway, he looked at me with those big, dark eyes. "You don't believe me, do you?" he said. "Well, I don't blame you. Sometimes you don't know what to believe, what not to believe. But I'll tell you a story. Maybe then you'll believe me."

He told me he was a twin, the one born first. It was a difficult delivery. His twin brother ended up brain damaged, was slow learning to talk, never reached normal intelligence. His brother attended special classes. He did only menial jobs, died in his late twenties of a heart defect.

"I guess I'm grateful," Doctor Z said, "grateful I made it okay. I'm grateful to the Lord. Grateful to my brother." He stopped and thought for a second, like he was meditating about it. For me, this was a new side of him. "I loved... I love my brother," he said, and hesitated again. He said he didn't *blame* himself for his brother. "But I feel I owe it to him to be something special, to give something back to society, to be more than just a rich suburban dentist with a condo in Florida."

I was moved by his story, and said so. I wanted to give him something in return. I told him about myself. I'd never told any of the girls, but I wanted to tell him.

My father left when I was a baby. My mother was alcoholic. She didn't know how to take care of me, didn't even send me to school when I turned six. She didn't allow me outside to play. Everything in our apartment was painted a light brown: kitchen, living room, bathroom, my room.

There was a clear, dark blue ash tray I made into a ship on the rug. I pretended to go on cruises, to places like Miami and Coney Island.

I was hungry a lot. I would tell my mother, "I'm hungry," and she would say, "Okay, we'll eat." "In a minute," she'd say. But then often as not, we wouldn't.

When a social worker finally discovered me, I was classified as retarded. My mother was declared incompetent. My father was long gone, so I ended up in a state residential school. Probably I was better off there than at home, but some things I had at home I lost. For instance, the blue ash tray — I guess when they moved everything, they didn't realize it was my toy. I stayed in the residential school until I was 14. I'd never been to a real school, and when a volunteer came and read to us, I learned to read looking over her shoulder. When I was finally tested correctly, I was put into a normal foster home. I did fine, graduated from high school, even went to junior college, earned credits toward a psychiatric aide certificate. Actually it was nurse's aide, but when I go on I plan to specialize in psychiatric. Everything's been okay since. One of these days I'm going back, going to finish that certificate.

Anyway, I told him all this — the whole story, just like I'm telling it now. When I finished, Doctor Z didn't seem to know how to react. Maybe it made him uncomfortable. I guess I must have cried when I told it. I suppose it was the first time I really opened up to anybody. Before that, I was mostly concerned about him, about how I could support him in his work, what I could do to make *him* feel better.

He said he didn't mean to make me all emotional. I tried to explain it was okay, but he didn't want to hear it, just wanted the conversation to be over.

I don't know what he thought. I suppose he thought what I'd done, what I went through, was courageous, or lucky. Was I lucky, or unlucky? I don't even know myself. At any rate, things weren't the same after that. I still loved him, wanted him, but he changed. He became more and more busy with his other patients. We only saw each other twice after that conversation. He was even more quiet than before — almost withdrawn. Then he stopped making dates with me. He avoided me completely, put me off if I tried to call him. I thought, Well, I'm a strong person. All I've been through, I can take it. He'll come back, I thought.

I was still working it all out when one week he didn't show up at the hospital for appointments. Rumors started that he was in some sort of trouble. Overnight all the plants disappeared from the clinic. The next week a new dentist showed up.

Of course they did their best to cover it up, but the story leaked out bit by bit. Supposedly they found out Doctor Z was molesting other patients. He probably wouldn't have been found out, but a parent needed one of the patients to sign a paper, to establish guardianship. Evidently there was a will, some money involved. The patient told her mother about Doctor Z, said she was married to him, wanted him to get a share of the money.

Apparently he'd spread around the story about his twin, but it turned out he didn't even *have* a twin brother. He was an only child. There were also rumors about trouble he'd had in dental school, interning at a welfare clinic in Boston. Supposedly, back then, a woman filed charges: it had to do with her 13-year-old daughter. On that occasion, he got off without even a censure, got his license and everything. This time he got fired. People said he would probably lose his license.

I felt bad for the other patients, of course. Gwendolyn, for example. I feel sure she wasn't involved with him in any way — at least she never said so. But he'd worked on her, I mean she'd had work done on her teeth. You know, she really respected him. It shook her when all this broke. In fact, what happened to Doctor Z probably pushed Gwendolyn over the edge. At any rate, it's what made her come to me for help. Well, I did what I could, what I thought was best. You have to understand the hospitals then, the environment.

On top of everything else, I felt bad for Doctor Z. Was it because of me he did this? Because I told him my story? Because of our breaking up? Some of the attendants said he didn't molest any patients, but a patient with a crush on him had started the rumor, then other patients picked up on it. I still don't know. Mostly, I felt bad he'd ruined his career, right when he was doing so much good.

For that matter, I felt bad for myself. I felt stupid I'd told him my story. You tell a story like mine to someone, you more or less *give* yourself to that person. It's a matter of trust.

Then again, I suppose I learned from it. I'd like to believe I came out of it okay. I'd even like to believe it made me a better person. But then, who knows what to believe, and what not to believe?

Or how much of this to tell Doctor Woods? How much of this will she believe? What will she think? For example, would she have believed Doctor Z's story? Would she have believed that about his twin brother, about why he worked so hard? Would she have believed he was helping patients, doing good for them?

Around here, of course, it's fashionable to be cynical. It's what everybody says: No, they wouldn't have believed it; they would have seen through it. That's what my friend Marie said, that she knew Doctor Z "wasn't doing you no good," to use her expression. This was based on her watching every single episode of *This Woman's Life*, I suppose.

Well, it's easy to say that, after the fact. It's easy to be smug. And that's what I really hate, the smugness. People who haven't been *in* the situation, but who think they have it all figured out. It makes me want to scream.

And why should Doctor Woods be any different? She can sit in judgment, her Harvard Med School on the wall. This and that residency. I saw it all written up in the hospital bulletin when she was hired. But what does she know, except what she hears from me? What does she know about me? About my story? For all she knows, my story is made up, too. For all she knows, I molested patients.

For all anybody knows, I kept Gwendolyn with me at nights, after Doctor Z left. Made her spend nights with me, do the things I knew were best for her. Wouldn't that give her a feeling of security, make her feel loved? Doesn't everybody need that: to feel loved?

Maybe *I* outsmarted the nurses. Maybe *I* stocked up on pills. Maybe Gwendolyn swallowed *my* whole supply. Maybe I even gave them to her. How would anybody know?

Well, they can all think what they want. It isn't like they know a better way. Even today, with all the new drugs, I'd like to know how many patients Doctor Woods has cured? How many has the whole bunch of them cured? They all know so much, driving their little maroon Volvos with the skis on top, how come somebody didn't cure Gwendolyn? It's not as easy as on TV, that's why.

Anyway, whatever I tell Doctor Woods, she has no proof anything really happened, and I'm not saying it did. What I just said about Gwendolyn? And Doctor Szczepaniak? It's almost straight from TV — *This Woman's Life*. Seriously, I'm surprised anybody falls for it. Even if I swore it happened, who knows whether my story is true or not? Who knows what's a true story and what isn't? Maybe Doctor Woods should watch more TV, so she'd know the difference.

But I'll still talk to her. The main thing is: stick to the subject, don't skip around.

Tales of Destruction

Nothing worse than these meetings where people stand up in front and tell their sad stories. Tales of destruction, I call them: how they wrecked this or that, hurt the ones they loved, and so on. Well, don't worry: my story isn't like that. There's no destruction; nobody gets hurt.

Week before Halloween, my ex-wife called: How is she supposed to get Joey to come home at a reasonable hour on Halloween? "Hell, I say, the next day is Saturday. What's the big rush for him to be home?" Which means of course I have no morals, no interest in my own son, don't care what happens to him. She has to do it all herself, and so on.

Which couldn't be further from the truth, I care about him, I care about his grades, I care about his education, I care about his health. I went to every one of his football games, which she refuses to attend, afraid he'll get hurt. Him of all people, tough as he is! And what an arm that kid has on him for a ten-year-old! Hauls back and flings thirty-yard passes without blinking an eye.

Anyway, when she finally shuts up I offer a solution. "The day after Halloween is Saturday. I'll take Joey and his friend what's-his-name" — "Mark," she says — "him and Mark to New York. It'll be an education," I tell her. "Joey's been bugging me about the Turbotrain: comes down from Montreal, we can pick it up in New Haven. On one condition," I say: "provided he is in at a reasonable hour on Halloween."

She thinks this over. "What's a reasonable hour?" she wants to know. "Whatever you say," I tell her. "Well it's only the second year he's gone out on Halloween by himself." She thinks eight-thirty isn't unreasonable. No ten-year-old kid should be out this and that late, and so on. "It's up to you," I say. "Whatever you tell him. But you have to stick to it," I say. "Enforce it." Which is a joke, her enforcing *anything,* you should see it. "Anyway," I tell her, "if he gets home late, just leave a message on my answering machine and the trip is off."

"Why answering machine?" she wants to know. "Where will you be?" (It's been over two years and she still snoops around about where I'm going!) I tell her, "A party at some friends," to which she for once can't think up an answer, so we close the deal. "If you don't call," I tell her, "I'll pick them up at six a.m. sharp, so we can be in New Haven by the time the Turbotrain swings through there at eight-thirty. *But remember,"* I tell her. "I know," she says, "I've got to enforce it. Don't worry," she says.

So I go to my party Halloween night, which is a great time, which the main thing I remember is this girl Linda, one of the telemarketing people at work, has on this mouse costume and there was some game, something to do with maraschino cherries, which is a digression, I'll keep it short.

Okay. Except just to say, that's my belief, that party shows my philosophy about booze, for me it's just fun, a good time, a few laughs. I'm not one of these angry types. I never laid a hand on my ex-wife or the kid, never got into it with anybody at work. Just a good time, a few laughs. Which is what separates me from these sorry individuals at the meetings, their confessions, their self-pity. Which is why I don't go. I say, Why make it worse? What's to confess? What's to pity? But back to the story.

After I got home from the party I never even checked the answering machine and of course wouldn't you know it, the alarm didn't go off. Still, when she called, it was only ten till seven at that, but of course, she wanted to be hurt about something. "I thought you said six a.m. sharp," and so on. To which I said, "What are you complaining about? He got home on time, didn't he?" Ha! Was I dreaming?

This time her excuse was: Mark's parents had told him nine o'clock. (Can you believe it? She didn't even coordinate with Mark's parents?) Now Mark and his old man are over there waiting, and so on, and all about how embarrassed she is, how embarrassed Joey is (which is a joke: Joey of all people couldn't care less), and if I cared the least bit I would do this and that, and so on.

When I get over there, old man what's-his-name, Mark Senior, is there with a corn cob up his rear end. "Sure you're okay to drive down there?" And so on. I feel like saying, "Do you want a breathalyzer?" But I say, "Sure, I'm okay, no problem, just the alarm didn't go off." Ha, ha, he knows how that is, and so on. I think: I'll bet you do, Dumbass.

So we start off, and I take U.S. 1, which is more direct than 95. On the road it turns out Joey has his school thermos she's filled with black coffee and he offers me a cup. Can you believe it? Another one of her strategies to make me look like some kind of animal. Of course it's not his fault, and I say, "Thanks, I'll let you know if I need it."

So that goes fine until I guess somewhere around Hopkinton there was some construction and maybe I nodded off or something, but before I know it, I'm off to the side of the road in mud. I get out, up over my shoes in mud. The car: almost up to the hubcaps, and so on.

And this gets around to the point of the story. A lot of people, that would have been it. *Oh, Jesus, we've had an accident, we can't go, and so on.* But hey, I made a promise, I said New York, that's where we're going. I told the kids, sit tight, and half a mile up the road is a service station takes Master Card, and the guy pulls us out. No big deal. My philosophy is: you've got kids, you make a promise, you've got to set an example for them. Not just Joey, but Dumbass' kid too. We *all* owe it to *all* kids. People always want to get on you, drag you out to these imbecile meetings, the confessions, and so on. But the bottom line is: do you keep your promises? Believe me, Dumbass would have called the whole thing off at that point.

Anyway, the guy pulls us out of the mud and we get into New Haven at quarter past ten, just in time for the 11 a.m. to Penn Station, which is a clunker, stops at every village of five-hundred or more, but the kids don't mind, they still love it. And we all have a few good laughs over the conductor on the train who is giving me these looks with regard to my shoes which are pretty well wrecked and mud drying here and there on the bottoms of my trousers.

So we're in the City by three-fifteen, take in a Chinese restaurant which has I swear these sixteen-ounce Mai Tais. I take the kids to and from in a cab, and they love that, too. The Empire State Building is right there, so we do that, and there's a coin-operated telescope which I let them both do that, and so on. Not only it's an education but they love every minute of it. Joey wants to know about the Ground Zero memorial and the new World Trade Center and the other kid says he heard about some exhibit in the New York Times Building. "Some of those things we'll do the next time," I say. Which is fine because they both have to take a leak anyway.

Back at Penn Station there's perverts lounging around the men's room, so I give the kids money to use a stall and don't stop to wash your hands and quit staring and we're on the six-thirty out of there in the club car.

When I'm driving back home from New Haven Joey offers his thermos of coffee again which it's not his fault, she drums this into him. But I tell him, "Thanks, I'm fine."

Also I tell him, regarding the mud incident and the car and so on he doesn't have to mention that to his mother, which of course Joey fully understands, but what I really am getting across without saying it is the other kid is not to mention it to Dumbass. So I hope that sinks in but kids nowadays who knows. Actually as we let the other kid out at his house I get laughing to myself thinking of Dumbass' reaction if the kid *does* tell him. *Mud?! What mud?! What tow truck?!*

When I let Joey off I don't get out so I won't have to explain the muddy shoes and so on. But Joey, going up the front steps — I can tell he's had a great time.

Except right before he goes in the house he hauls back and flings his thermos bottle up into the front tree as far as he can and doesn't even watch as it bounces down through the branches and pops open, spreading black coffee on the front sidewalk.

Jesus! I think. His mother's temper. But better he lets it out that way than shooting up dope or something.

Anyway, it's only a ten-dollar thermos bottle. Like I say: No destruction. Nobody gets hurt. We all have a few laughs. Everybody lives happily ever after. Hey! It's an Education.

Jake's American Dream

All the plane crashes in the news had started Jake thinking about the Philippines again. Actually, he had been back from the Philippines, back from the Air Force, nineteen years. His first week back he started working for the Americo brothers.

"I ran the motor pool at Clark Air Force Base," he told Richie Americo the day he talked to him about a job at International Auto Parts.

Richie didn't need to hear it. He pushed the yellow job application aside, put an arm around Jake's shoulders. "Jackie, hey, we want you here. You're like part of the family."

Jake had gone to Toll Gate High with Richie's kid brother, Ronnie. Four nights before graduation Ronnie crashed his brand new Corvette into the Warwick Avenue viaduct.

Talking to Jake about Ronnie, Richie always got emotional. "You were close to Ronnie," he told Jake. "You're like a brother to us."

Jake wasn't exactly *close* to Ronnie. Let's say he *knew* Ronnie. One semester Jake was shop partners with Ronnie. Actually, Jake pretty much carried Ronnie through that semester of shop. All due respect, but Jake thought Ronnie didn't try. It was like Ronnie never knew what a privilege it was to be part of the Americo family, never knew that being rich was more than just expensive clothes and new cars, never knew that more was expected.

The Corvette was Ronny's graduation present. It was the third car he wrecked since he turned 16. Ronnie was the youngest of the five Americo brothers. The oldest was a lawyer. The next one managed the family's assets. He was an accountant. Richie and Vito were next; they were International Auto Parts. Who knows where Ronnie would have fit in, had he lived.

Anyway, Richie hired Jake on, and Jake became family. Richie showed him stock levels. Showed him how to ring discounts for each of the dealers coming in. Showed him how to use the tables. For example, you need a Pontiac muffler. Maybe a Chevy will fit. Or fan belts, wiper blades, the same. It was all in the tables.

Mostly Richie taught him to take care of the dealers. Especially the big ones like Ocean State Exxon, where there were six repair bays, or Elmwood Sunoco, with a mechanic on duty 24 hours. That's where you make it or break it — the dealers.

Richie showed him. And Jake learned. Within two weeks he knew the names of all the dealers, knew who worked where, knew what they ordered, knew their discounts by heart. They liked that: the personal touch. Jake got to where he could even quote the tables by heart, but he always double-checked. Hey, if Jake wrote it up for you, you knew it was right.

Jake was glad Richie noticed all of this. "That's my boy," Richie would say. Richie introduced Jake to the old man. "Pop," Richie said, "you remember Jake." Jake didn't know if the old man would remember. "You remember Ronnie and Jake," Richie said, holding up two fingers together. "Ronnie and him were like this." The old man smiled and shook his hand. It made Jake feel part of the family.

Jake's own father had been gone since he was four, and after he came to work there Richie sort of adopted Jake. A month after starting to work Jake married his high school sweetheart, Agnes Pelletier. Richie was godfather to their oldest boy, Jackie Junior.

Jake always liked being with the Americo brothers. Nobody ever called it International Auto Parts. It was always: "So you work for the Americo Brothers." Everybody knew the Americo Brothers was a first-class operation, the major leagues.

Jake liked being part of the family, too, except he knew adopted wasn't the same as blood. Take Richie's cousin, Julio. You could tell Julio was blood. Eight years after Jake started, Julio graduated from Boston College. Julio got the new buyer's position that opened up. Jake had wanted buyer, but he stayed at the counter.

"Hey, that's okay!" he assured Richie. "I'll get my chances, don't worry! Julio can use the break. Boston College? That kid's a flash! You know? Julio's got promise!"

So Jake stayed mostly at the counter. Except, of course, the time he spent breaking Julio in on stock levels. Showing Julio how to ring discounts. Introducing Julio to the reps. He's going to be a buyer, he has to know the reps. You know? Ralph Silveira, from Seekonk. Donny from City Side. Arthur, from Consolidated, over on Douglas Pike.

No problem. Anyway, Arthur still gave Jake a punch in the shoulder when he came in on Tuesday mornings to get his order from Julio. And of course a calendar for Christmas. Is that a *calendar*, or what?

Then the new store opened in North Providence. Vito moved up to the new store. Richie made Jake retail manager. Richie grabbed him by the back of the neck and shook his hand good. "You son of a gun, Jackie. Remember you came in here from Vietnam? Mister ex-Marine? If Ronnie was only here to see you now. You guys would be so good together." Actually, it was the Air Force, Jake thought, and the Philippines. And nobody had called him "Jackie" since fourth grade. Well, whatever.

So Jake was retail manager, got a nice increase off that, too. Didn't see that much of Richie after that. Richie spent a lot of time getting Julio on track. Or else he was off at the North Providence store. No problem. Jake took charge. "I got things under control here, Richie. Go to the new store. I'll keep your boy Julio out of trouble, see he doesn't screw up the Empire order again."

Agnes got nervous about this kind of talk, didn't like Jake to make fun of Julio. Julio was *family*, not just a guy.

"Are you kidding?" he said to Agnes. "Richie can take a joke. Richie and me, we go back. Agnes, for Christ sake, I went to school with *Ronnie*. Richie thinks of me as family."

Anyway: Agnes was good, took good care of the kids. Jackie Junior was six. The Princess was four. Brian, the baby, seven months. The *baby*, for Christ sake. *Monster man!* You want to see a middle linebacker? You ought to see the legs on that kid. And the lungs.

Agnes put the baby in with Jackie Junior. Jackie Junior needed a brother, right? And the Princess had her own room. So the house was busting at the seams. Toys, doll clothes, the Little Lady Makeup Kit. And the baby in his walker through the middle of it all.

Anyway, it was better than the rented tenement on Crystal Boulevard, where Jake grew up. His mother lived there until her stroke, right up until she went into the hospital. She had her friends there, didn't really want to move. True, it hadn't been that great a life for Jake's mother. She had to push hard. Waitress at The Villa. Sometimes till almost midnight. Then see that Jake was out of the house at five for the paper route. But they survived, didn't they?

After his mother left the hospital, Medicare picked up the tab for only three weeks at Charles Manor Rehab. Even then she used a walker, had trouble talking. She's my mother, Jake told Agnes.

"Don't worry, Honey," said Agnes, "We'll find a way."

To keep from crying, Jake had to grab hold of Agnes, hold her close for a minute.

By then his mother's apartment was cleaned out, all her essentials in one black footlocker. Jake put the rest in boxes and made room for it in the attic.

Jackie Junior and Brian moved to the basement, where Jake partitioned off a room, put up paneling. The Princess kept her room, of course.

Agnes got the heavier window shades for Jackie Junior's old room, to keep out the early morning light. Jake's mother said she could hear the birds singing already at four-thirty. The footlocker fit in one corner. Her walker by the chest of drawers.

At first Agnes was afraid Brian was too young to sleep in the basement. He was three and a half. Are you kidding? At three and a half Jake was helping the kid next door with his paper route! Still, every morning Jake and Agnes woke up with Brian in bed between them. We'll find a way, said Agnes. And that's how they ended up getting the new house.

Sure, they had to stretch a little, but it ended up a good investment. Plus they sold the old house at a good profit. And Agnes wanted to work anyway, when Brian started kindergarten. The year they got the new house Jackie Jr. was in middle school. Carla was nine. It was time for Agnes to get out, do the things she'd wanted to do. She went to work evenings to help with the mortgage payments on the new house. *Big* mortgage payments. Back then interest rates were crazy. Bad timing. Worst market ever. Maybe refinance in two, three years.

Anyway, it was a bigger house, right? Nothing fancy. Two baths. The other house only had one. The extra bedroom. Nice neighborhood.

Agnes worked in the fabric store. She had always liked to sew. Liked fabrics. Liked people. She waited on customers. Answered questions. Actually, if people would just *read*. The patterns spell it out: A, B, C.

Meanwhile, Jake was still at the counter. Still retail manager, but doing a lot more. When Julio told Richie they needed another delivery van, Jake reworked all the routes so they could still handle it with just the three. Saved twenty-eight grand there for the Americo brothers, on the new van alone, another twenty, twenty-two a year for a new driver. Plus kept the other drivers on the move, instead of paying them nine-fifty an hour to sit around in Mister Donut drinking coffee and talking to the girls. And it was Jake's idea to put in the computer so you could put your hand on what you needed without holding up your customer half the morning.

In fact, who ran the place? The old man? Jake didn't see the old man any more. I mean, he presented Jake his fifteen-year pin. They had a cake with fifteen candles. But other than this, nobody really saw the old man any more.

So who did run the place? Richie? Sure, when he was there. But Richie had his condo now. Spent half the winter in Florida, him and Vito both. So who did dealers talk to when there was a problem? How about vendors? Reps? How about Donny? How about Arthur, from Consolidated? Who did they ask to double-check the orders after Julio signed them? Jake, of course.

They made no bones about it. Hey, with orders, you're talking *money. Commissions!* This isn't fun and games. You said Julio signed it? Good luck, baby!

And that's what finally did it: Julio. Didn't Jake take the belt order back to him on three different occasions, tell him you couldn't just write *837*? You had to write *837A, 837B, 837C*: whatever you were running out of. Richie always said, and Jake remembered, "A car can't run without a belt." There was even a cartoon, a guy trying to run, his pants falling down. *A car can't run without a belt.* Did it take a degree from Boston College to understand this?

And didn't Jake know it would happen? One Friday afternoon, five minutes before closing, Frank from Sullivan's SuperService called, had to have an 837C, and there was none in stock. Mister Boston College had knocked off at three o'clock to play golf. Richie was in Aruba or someplace, hadn't shown his face in a week. Jake called the North Providence store, couldn't even get an answer. It was the first time in nineteen years Jake couldn't fill an emergency belt order. It sure as hell was no way to treat one of the dealers.

So when Jake had a shot at leasing the first store in the new plaza on Airport Road, he decided to go out on his own, open up his own business. He decided to go for it. "You'll be the flagship," the developer told Jake. "A solid business!" He made a fist and held it up.

It was the perfect spot to set up his own business. Good retail counter space. Close to everything. Close to *the dealers*, baby. Jake should know, right? Nineteen years in the business. He knew retail alone wouldn't do it. You need the dealer business.

So: Jake set up the financing: a second mortgage. Home Equity Line, they call it. Actually, it wasn't that easy to get. First Union was out of the question. For years they'd banked for the Americos: the old man, *his* old man. They would have wanted Richie to countersign. Can you imagine? Richie, will you countersign for Jake? Jake wants to go in competition. Jake wants to put your smooth ass out of business, Richie. Jake wants to put that cream puff Julio on the street.

Liberty National was the same, though. Rhode Island Trust: the same. The first question they asked Jake: Mr. Florio, don't you work for the Americo Brothers? Richie? Vito? Oh, the utmost discretion, Mr. Florio. We understand completely, Mr. Florio.

Hey, screw 'em. He finally got the loan through Eastern Trust. Screw Liberty National. Screw Rhode Island Trust. Screw their discretion.

Eastern Trust had a brand new store-front office on Warwick Avenue. Three teller machines. On-line banking. A web site with all the latest CD rates. Pushing the Home Equity Line. Jake decided not to mention Airport Parts to Eastern Trust. No need to talk about a startup business. All that crap about risk. Money is money, right? A $100,000 line of credit. That ought to do it, right? Jake wouldn't use it all at first, of course. The basic franchise, for starters. That included initial stock levels. Plus the few extra things still on order. He would use his own van for deliveries, so that helped.

All Jake needed was enough business to pay it back month by month. Thirty-eight hundred. Five thousand a month clear, maybe. That plus living expenses. And their first mortgage.

Sure, Agnes worried. What if this happened? What if that happened? But every family needs one to worry, one to move ahead. So let's don't get on Agnes. Agnes signed the second mortgage, worked her little fanny off.

You want to get *on* somebody, get on Donny and Arthur. After all, they represented the major parts lines, and Jake counted on them to be his suppliers.

Jake put out feelers to them when he was still working on the loan, negotiating the lease. I mean feelers. Jake couldn't just lean across the counter and say: Hey, Donny, I'm going in business for myself.

So when Donny found out Jake was setting up shop on Airport Road, he told Jake about the five-mile limit. "I'd like to have your business, Jake, but you're only a mile, mile and a half from the Americo Brothers."

Five-mile limit? Are you kidding me? How come I never heard of any five-mile limit?

Arthur, the same. "We've got to think about past and future ties," said Arthur. Are you serious, Arthur? What kind of talk is that, Arthur? Past ties? Nineteen years isn't past ties?

Well, screw *them!* Arthur, and Consolidated, and Donny and the whole bunch of them could take their frigging calendars and stuff them. Jake wouldn't hang that crap around anyway. Are you serious? For his daughter to see?

Anyway, so much for Consolidated. So much for Donny. Jake did better. You wouldn't believe what you find when you have to look around. You ever hear of SaveMinder? SaveMinder parts? Do you believe all that about Mr. Goodwrench parts? Mr. Good *Buck*, that's what Jake called them. SaveMinder came in at forty, forty-five percent off the name brands. We're talking *money* here, my friend. This isn't fun and games.

Another thing about SaveMinder was: a full-service outfit. They arranged the insurance. They gave you a sign. Furnished their own auto parts software. They arranged towels and soap for the bathroom. You didn't have fifty or sixty guys nickel-and-diming you to death.

Of course Donny never heard of SaveMinder. Donny? Donny grew up on Oaklawn Avenue, only been out of Rhode Island maybe twice in his life. Donny could never have found SaveMinder. Donny couldn't have found his ass with both hands and a flashlight.

Actually, the dealers would eat up SaveMinder. You run a garage or a gas station, it's a business, just like Airport Parts. Just like Jake. You gotta watch your margins.

Let Jake Florio Help You Save With SaveMinder. That's what Jake said in his mailing to the dealers. *Bring This Postcard In For A Free Gift. Have A Free Coffee And Danish With Jake.* The dealers all knew Jake. They'd be there.

But it's funny, the reactions you get. Jake talked to Dave, at Pilger's Citgo. Dave inherited the station from his old man. "What are you doing it for, Jake? All the grief, the risk. Why would anybody leave the Americo Brothers?"

Jake just smiled. "It's the American dream," he told Dave. If you have to ask, Jake thought, you'd never understand. Of course, that's Dave. Dave didn't know what it was like to struggle. Dave thought he was doing you a favor to take his coffee cup off the cash register long enough to ring up your sale. Jake didn't even bother to explain to Dave how using SaveMinder would increase his margins.

* * * *

So, finally, opening day! Jake woke up this morning at 5 a.m. When he first saw the clock it took him back to when he was a kid, getting up early to deliver papers. Then he thought about opening day, and went to take his shower.

The kids were still asleep when Jake left the house at six. You run a business, it's up early, he told Agnes. Especially on opening day.

He was out the door, almost forgot the lunch Agnes fixed. She ran it out to him. "You go on," she told Jake. "I'll put the garage door down for you." Mornings, Agnes didn't usually come outside, but today she stood in the driveway, waved to Jake until he turned the corner.

He'd hired Agnes's niece, Heather, to do the coffee and Danish for the opening. And pass out the free gifts. Heather had it all set up at seven o'clock sharp, all the free gifts laid out ready, but Jake asked *her* to hand them out, not just have guys come in scooping them up. Actually the free gifts aren't bad. Key chains. SaveMinder logo. The motto: *Save with SaveMinder.* Jake's phone number on the back.

Frigging phones, that's another story. Right now they're tied together instead of three separate lines. Phone guy'll be back today and straighten it out. Jake was busy stocking shelves when the phone guy left, didn't have a chance to check out the lines. So now when a call comes in, all three phones ring, and he's on all three lines. Who needs three phones, anyway? That's another

SaveMinder requirement, unfortunately. "Our standard setup," the SaveMinder regional guy told him. As if Jake didn't know anything about phones. Anyway, that will all get straightened out. And hopefully the computer will stop going down every time Heather tries to enter a new customer.

Outside, there's red, white, and blue pennants across the front of the store, just under the Airport Parts sign and the SaveMinder logo. The other three stores in the shopping center are empty. But in one a painter has laid out a tarpaulin on the unfinished floor, and is stirring a can of yellow paint.

For a moment Jake imagines Airport Parts filling all four stores in the plaza. One for truck parts, another for imports. One mostly for retail. And how about *www.AirportParts.com*, featuring *Special-Of-The-Month*? Hey, why not? Who's to stop him?

The developer told Jake confidentially that a significant client was ready to sign on the dotted line for the second store in the plaza, next to Jake. Serious walk-in business, he told Jake. But Agnes heard it might be an exercise studio.

Whatever, thinks Jake. He's his own boss now. Whoo, boy! His own boss.

There was actually one customer on Friday, even though today is opening day. Guy wandered in and wanted new blades for his 5-year-old pickup. Jake had just unpacked them and put them on the shelf. Is that an omen or what? Anyway, you can bet Jake sold them to him, opening day or not. Gave him a ten percent discount because he was the first customer. Jake taped the pink copy of the slip to the wall behind the counter. Number 0001. Now the writeup thing is sitting there with 0002, waiting for the first *real* customer.

Actually there have been a few this morning, if you can call them customers. A lot more if it weren't for the traffic. Expected a lot of the dealers to drop by for their coffee and Danish.

Talk about omens. Guess what comes on the news last night. You know the stealth bomber? Tomorrow, the news says, the stealth bomber makes its first and only landing at Providence. *Ever.* And it's Jake's Opening Day!

This morning, driving in, Jake hears about the stealth bomber on the radio. The traffic 'copter on WPRO is telling everybody: your best view of the stealth bomber is from Airport Road. On 94 HJY it's the same: the stealth bomber's landing pattern is right over Airport Road. WKMZ: Airport Road. *Everybody:* Airport Road.

It's like the stealth bomber is paying the rent on Airport Road, not Jake.

So, it was already busy at twenty after six when Jake got there. Heather was almost late because of it. She said, "What's all the traffic?"

"*All the traffic?* Are you kidding me? Look out there *now:* wall to wall, bumper to bumper."

By quarter till eight every mother in Rhode Island is here with a car full of kids. From the looks of it, quite a few are skipping school to see the stealth bomber. Senior citizens. Guys skipping *work.* Cars have pulled off all along the side of Airport Road. The rest is gridlock. Both directions. Most of the drivers not even *trying* to move. Just looking. Everybody looking.

No dealer is going to fight *this* to get over here. Nineteen years or not! Well, except for Souza's Chevron, just across the street on Airport Road, about twenty yards down. Their entire crew was over here. The minute Heather got the coffee and Danish set up, of course. They just walked across the street through the traffic. Greased up quite a few of Jake's red-white-and-blue paper napkins, too. What can you say? One free Danish per dealer? Hey, come on: it's opening day.

Manny runs Souza's Chevron, but he doesn't get in over there till 8:30 or 9:00. Sonny was with them, though. Sonny is Manny's kid. Jake handed Sonny the free gift. "Does your old man have an order written up for me?" Jake asked. Nice and friendly, of course. Sonny smiled. "I hear you left the Americo Brothers," he said. No shit, Sonny. What a genius!

When they left, grease everywhere! Jesus! Quite a dent in the Danish, too. Jake got Heather to take the Windex and do over the counters, and get rid of all the greasy napkins. Then rearrange the Danish. Spread them out.

Jake has Heather turn away a teenage girl in a bathing suit who wants to use the bathroom. Must think this is the beach or something. I'm sorry. You have to draw the line.

Earlier Jake let a mother and a baby use it. Big mistake. Immediately twelve more kids and mothers came in. One of them even asked if the coffee and Danish were free.

Now, the answer is: no bathroom facilities. Period. Jake printed it on a piece of cardboard and taped *it* on the wall behind the counter. You've got to have policies. Jake tells Heather to direct the bathroom people to Souza's Chevron. Across the street, about twenty yards down.

But that doesn't help the gridlock. Crazy! Jake wonders what would happen if he told people the stealth bomber was canceled. No, even better: The stealth bomber has crashed! Just walk out front and holler it, The stealth bomber has crashed! Maybe everybody would leave. How about: the stealth bomber has crashed, *and it's on television!* Would that do it, or what? *The stealth bomber has crashed! It's on television!* Everybody would go home to watch.

Speaking of crashes. How about insurance? Jake goes around the counter and roots in the cabinet where he's put his catalogs. Envelope marked *Insurance.* The policy. SaveMinder guy got it for him, through Northern Missouri Indemnity. How would Northern Missouri Indemnity like to know Airport Parts is in the landing pattern of the stealth bomber?

Jake sees something about earthquakes and natural disasters but can't find planes. Or airplanes, or air anything. Or crashes. Would it be under vehicles? No vehicles, either. He puts the policy back and walks outside. Pay your money, take your chances.

Outside, people are pointing to the sky across Airport Road. Sure enough, it's here, the stealth bomber is here, banking into its final approach. More people spot it. Kids holler out. Parents hoist them up. As he shades his eyes and looks up, the stealth bomber lines up straight for him.

Actually, at Clark it was nothing but B-52s, so Jake has never before seen the stealth bomber. It's like something out of Star Wars, its profile barely visible from head on. Just a pair of wings and no main fuselage holding them together.

Straight in it comes. Straight for Airport Parts. Half a mile away Jake realizes it will not be loud like the noisy waves of B52's returning to Clark. And only in the last split-second does he hear it, just as the mysterious set of wings whooshes its shadow over Airport Parts and sets down safely on runway 22L.

At that instant the sun slips behind a set of clouds, leaving the landscape dimmed, as if the shadow of the creatureless wings has stuck.

Jake watches the stealth bomber until it taxies off the runway, crawling along the ground toward the terminal. He surveys the traffic, which is at a standstill, blanketed by shadow, cemented together by the noise of car horns and kids' crying.

Maybe they'll get out of here now, Jake thinks. Maybe they'll get out of here, and then maybe some of the dealers will start coming in.

Jake tries to imagine the dealers coming in, driving up in their pickups, parking, heading for his front door. He imagines Manny, from Souza's Chevron, just across the street on Airport Road, about twenty yards down. He imagines Antone from over at Four Corners Texaco, Charlie from Ocean State Exxon. Even Dave, from Pilger's Citgo, inherited the station from his old man. Now that the stealth bomber has landed, Jake can even imagine Dave coming in.

But as he sees them in his mind — the dealers, Manny, Antone, Charlie, Dave, and a whole slew more behind them — he imagines them walking across his asphalt parking area here on Airport Road. They are wearing hard hats, carrying lunch pails. And when they look up, Jake doesn't see the faces of the dealers — Manny and Antone, Charlie and Dave. Instead he is taken back to the Philippines, the day one of the B52's crash landed. He sees the faces of the Filipino maintenance workers, that day. They had this superstition a B-52 crash would cause a nuclear explosion, radiation poisoning. Nothing anybody said could change their minds.

From the three maintenance hangars they pushed their way toward the gate at Clark Air Force Base, serious and quiet, as if they didn't want anyone to discover their secret. They clutched their lunch pails, pushed toward the gate, trying to get home before everything went up. They looked straight ahead, ignoring the rescue wagons screaming across the tarmac behind them.

Free Advice

Once a man called me to sell his business. He had a falling out with his wife. She was fooling around, or he was, I can't remember. He wanted to sell everything, divide it up, and get out of town.

I invited him out to my office, but we didn't talk about his business. We talked about his four kids — three teenagers, plus a boy just entering junior high. His daughter was just accepted at Rhode Island School of Design. He told me their youngest had breathing problems as an infant. During the night they both got up to check on him until he straightened out. We talked about his wife. Yes, he still loved her. And so on.

I asked if there was a possibility of his doing this and that, talking about thus and such with his wife. He appreciated my suggestions, and left with a whole new outlook. Apparently everything got patched up. He didn't sell his business after all.

When my partner heard, he left a note on my desk. *Congratulations, Doctor Freud!* it said. He attached a calculator tape showing the commission we missed on that deal.

But that's my partner. For my part, I felt pretty good. Things worked out well for the guy. More than that, I avoided preying on someone's misfortunes. And I felt like I made an impact.

My partner flips when he hears me talk this way. "I don't understand 'making an impact'?" he says. "Buying and selling businesses, arranging financing — *that's* making an impact!"

And of course he's right. We've done well the last twenty-odd years, but not by giving free advice. There have been a lot of changes in that time. Used to be you could be flexible, have a little fun, make a few dollars. Now there are rules against everything.

The guy with the four kids was a few years back. Afterward he called me occasionally to shoot the breeze. ("How's the marriage counseling, Doctor Freud?" my partner would ask me.) But I talked to the guy mostly about his business: they made blueprints, restored them, copied them. Now they digitized them, blending old tech and new. He had shops around Boston, up into New Hampshire. A half dozen vans going constantly. I once asked him what the secret to his success was.

"Silver," he said.

I thought I misunderstood. "Silver *what?*" I asked him.

"Silver," he repeated. "The metal." Apparently the most expensive component of photographic film is silver. The price of silver was over half his cost of sales. It controlled his margins, dictated his profit.

So when the big hullabaloo with silver prices first started, my partner and I were ready. While everybody else was going nuts over silver futures, we avoided the crowd, sold short a bunch of photographic stocks. When silver prices shot up, the stocks went down, and we picked up a bundle. After that my partner's Doctor Freud jokes eased up.

* * * *

I've stopped giving out free advice. And I've also stopped investing in start-up companies. After a bad experience I'm leaving that to the crazies. You run into enough craziness in the world without signing up for it! By craziness I mean venture capital. The Silicon Valley, high-tech variety: that's craziness. I've known venture capital guys who did not act crazy in real life. But if you showed them some high-tech deal, they got crazy. Better still: a *rumor* of a high-tech deal, and they wanted in. They're crapshooters. One guy I knew invested in every company with *laser* in the title. Another's main concern was whether the company's top executives were obese. Or whether the company's logo included the color orange. And so on. Some of them end up in Palm Springs, some on Skid Row.

So, no more start-up companies for me. My bad experience was Amaryllis Systems Corporation. If you've never heard of them, just have a drink in any of the old watering holes in Boston's financial district. You can always find someone who will talk about Amaryllis. Everybody has his own version of the story. Some claim they knew Maribeth Simon, the genius who started Amaryllis. Some knew Roger Brimley, the guy Maribeth hired to organize a sales force.

I knew them both. In fact, I brought them together — unfortunately.

Previously I had arranged the buyout of another company Roger worked for. He was VP for sales, but in reality he ran the place. At the time he was the hottest sales property in the enterprise computing industry. He brought this company from nothing to $450 million sales in only four years. His people were dedicated, worked long hours, lived, ate, and slept computer system sales to large businesses. They were fiercely loyal to Roger. By contrast, the owner was disengaged, spent half his time in Antigua, wanted to get his money out of the company and be done with it.

We eventually paid him $285 million. Ironically, Roger — after making the company what it was — got less than a few grand out of the deal, from some shares the owner gave him as a bonus one year.

I made up my mind Roger would get a better deal under the new owners, a company in Buffalo called Comprel.

"What's it to you?" my partner wanted to know. "Why can't this Roger look out for himself?" He said I was on a power trip.

Who knows what I was on? To me, it just didn't seem right. So I told the new owners there were a dozen or more companies waiting to give Roger some stock to lure him away. (Surely there were?)

As a result, they loaded Roger with enough stock options to make it worth his while.

"Joe Do Good!" my partner called me. But Roger was happy. The new owners were happy. And I was happy to see it all work out.

Off the record, this is what *I* mean when I say "have an impact." I did more than just put the deal together between the two companies. I stuck my neck out, not wanting to see Roger get screwed again. It paid off for everybody, and I felt I earned my commission check. *"Earned it?"* my partner would say. "You earned it by selling the business, not being some amateur guidance counselor!" (That's why I try not to discuss any of this around my partner.)

About the same time, I met Maribeth Simon — actually, got a letter from her. She was twenty-six, wanted to start a company. Just like that. She got our name by searching some Wall Street directory on the Web. My partner thought it was a great laugh, but I wanted to hear more.

Maribeth was completely engaging on the phone: her enthusiasm came right over the wires. She had invented a way to store mountains of seismic data in a company's data base, so it was secure yet available to the company's engineers and geologists, and had shaped this into an elaborate software system for oil exploration. She was working for Storage Systems Corporation then, and they were too busy going bankrupt to listen to her. She wrote software for Storage Systems, polished off her week's assignment in two or three hours, then spent the rest of the week playing around with her own ideas. But nobody paid attention.

We met for the first time at the Salt Lake City Airport. Talk about surprised! I don't buy into stereotypes, but someone that smart, you expect a female nerd, right? You don't expect a combination of a fashion model and that good-looking black-haired science correspondent on CNN. Plus a mind like a steel trap. She explained her ideas to me in layman's terms. I was impressed.

I called an MIT professor I knew, got him to talk to Maribeth. He reported back to me it was a sound idea. "You've got yourself a genius there," he told me. "How do I buy some of that stock?"

My partner and I weren't investing in start-up companies then, but I put Maribeth in touch with two venture capital guys I knew. "MIT claims she's a genius," I told them. Eventually both of them backed Maribeth, and she started Amaryllis Systems.

"So what's your finder's fee for that?" my partner chided.

"Life is more than finder's fees," I told him. Of course, he knows this. My partner and I go back 23 years, and we've been very successful. Part of our success is this: he keeps me from rooting through the trash, keeps my eye on the ball. On the other hand, I spot opportunities where he can't. We make a good team.

Maribeth kept in touch, and it looked like Amaryllis Systems was doing well. So when the second round of venture capital financing came around, I talked my partner into getting involved. We went in for twenty million, small potatoes compared to the big guys, but it was our first time.

Shortly after we became involved, Amaryllis got a grant from the Department of Energy, as well as a contract from Texaco for a prototype system. Things looked very good. Not only that, I was able to write off a trip to Salt Lake City every two or three months, get in some time on the slopes. When my partner complained, I reminded him of our "office" in Florida where he goes to play polo with Prince Charles and the captains of industry every winter.

In the meantime, back at Comprel, Roger was thriving with the new owners in Buffalo. His people doubled the company's sales the first year. I called Roger every month or so, got a good fix on Comprel's earnings every quarter before they were announced.

Just to be clear, I'm not talking any insider stuff here. Let's just say: I could tell. As a result I milked a few hundred grand out of Comprel options while Roger was there. Of course, if that was today, I'd have the feds all over me, wanting to ask me a million private questions about who knew what and when. That's why I say a lot of the fun has gone out of the business. Sometimes I think about moving to Antigua myself!

Anyway, Roger continued to do a bang-up job. Naturally Comprel was quite pleased with him. The following year, when their VP for sales took early retirement, they gave Roger the job. His picture was on the cover of the next issue of *eVenture*.

The same issue had a front-page spread on Amaryllis and Maribeth Simon. Pictures showed Maribeth regaling a bunch of Ph.D.'s at an oil-industry convention, a prototype system blinking away in a lab in Tulsa, the Texaco Star on the wall behind it. After the *eVenture* spread investors were breaking down the doors. The third round of venture capital was spoken for long before it hit the street.

Orders started to come in before the system went into production. It looked like things were taking off faster than expected. If anything, too fast. At the next investment meeting in Salt Lake City, one of the new investors asked to see a sales plan.

Maribeth blinked, and I knew from her expression she didn't know what a sales plan was. Whoo boy, I thought, looking toward the exit. I'd seen too many situations like this: a brilliant scientist starts a business, develops a great product, but can't get a sales organization set up, can't run the business end of it.

Maribeth had a great product, but no sales organization to speak of. Until then Maribeth was personally involved in each of the sales Amaryllis made. She dealt directly with the research departments at the major oil companies, spoke the language of the seismologists and research VP's. Now, with business starting to accelerate, it was clear Maribeth had to choose between being the genius behind the tech aspects of the company and being the chief salesperson.

Clear to everyone but Maribeth. She didn't put that much stock in what she called a *"formal* sales force," felt the system pretty much sold itself, an engineer could answer questions about it better than a salesman. Later I found out the few sales people she had were second-stringers, flunkies for the engineers. They answered the phone, maintained a delivery schedule, and made sure the brochures were updated and spelled right. At the meeting, there were a few more questions about sales, none of which Maribeth handled very well.

I kept quiet then, but made up my mind to call Roger the minute I got back. I knew he was the right person.

My partner hissed like a water moccasin when I said I was trying to put Roger in touch with Maribeth. "The job counselor is at it again," he said. I told him the job counselor was trying to protect our twenty-million bucks.

He said he appreciated my solicitude for the money, but wished I would leave recruiting to someone who knew what he was doing. He reminded me I couldn't even *explain* the Amaryllis system, much less recruit someone to sell it.

"I'm no scientist," I said.

"Good!" he said. "At least you've decided that."

You've got to take my partner with a grain of salt. I called Roger anyway, and it was the right thing to do.

"I still like my job," he said, "but it's mostly managing other sales managers." He missed working directly with the sales people, missed the customer contact.

Roger liked the idea of the sales position at Amaryllis, where he could develop his own organization almost from scratch. He visited Maribeth in Salt Lake City the following week. He got the full treatment. Maribeth's enthusiasm was contagious, and there was an air of excitement among the employees. They'd received over eight-thousand new orders since the *eVenture* spread, and the adrenalin was flowing. Maribeth took time to explain the system. Roger seemed pleased he understood it all. He sounded ready to sign with them.

He said Maribeth assured him a free hand in setting up the sales organization. They stayed up past midnight talking about it. Within two months Roger was in Salt Lake City as Maribeth's VP for sales.

Maribeth escorted him into the next investors' meeting. Only two weeks on the job, Roger presented a crisp but thorough overview of sales plans. Already he had an intimate knowledge of the Amaryllis System, the likely users, best sales prospects. He projected good increases in sales for the next two quarters. He was encouraging but candid: listed strengths and weaknesses of the product, principal competitors, *their* strengths and weaknesses. It was a sharp contrast to the fumbling embarrassment of the previous meeting. Maribeth beamed at Roger throughout. Glad to be out of the spotlight, I thought, able to focus on designing the next system. What a combination!

There was an air of euphoria after the meeting. Several of the venture capital guys crowded around Roger, pursued issues he raised. Roger was at ease answering their questions. Others talked among themselves about the presentation, repeating points from the slide copies Roger passed out. People congratulated Maribeth on the team she was building. Two or three guys, hearing I brought Roger on board, clapped me on the back.

I caught up with Roger in the hall, gave him a thumbs up. "Good show," I said. "Keep this up, you'll make rookie of the year." He was still glowing from the excitement of the meeting and the presentation.

He turned down my offer of lunch. Said he was having lunch with Maribeth. No problem, I assured him. But then he seemed to want to explain. "A *working* lunch," he said, unconvincingly.

On the plane back to Boston I thought, *whatever works!* If Roger and Maribeth were attracted to one another, so what? Wouldn't they work better together?

The tunnel from the airport was jam-packed, as usual, and I didn't get back to the office until five after seven. My partner was just leaving for the night. He wanted to know whether Amaryllis had solved the problem with their sales organization.

"They're getting a helluva team put together out there," I told him.

"They'd better!" he said. He offered that he'd feel considerably more comfortable if I were betting the twenty-million at the crap tables in Vegas. My partner has always been a skeptical person. I decided not to tell him about the working lunch. He would have pointed out Roger was married.

* * * *

I had to miss the next investors' meeting, but got the handouts faxed to me. Roger's sales projections were right on target, but the company was spending too much money, so the loss for the quarter was a million and a half more than expected — as if nobody was keeping tabs. A projection showed the break-even point eight months out. Not bad for a company that new — *if* they could now pay more attention to their expenses and get the bottom line straightened out. That depended on Roger and Maribeth working together – "working" being the operant word.

By chance I saw Roger six weeks later. We ended up in the same boarding area at LaGuardia, waiting for different flights. I almost didn't recognize him. His collar was unbuttoned and he'd gained weight. "How's it going out there?" I asked.

"No problem," he said. "Never a dull moment." He smiled, but looked beat. Stress City, I thought. I knew Roger well enough to be worried.

I worried for him, but I also thought about what my partner said about Las Vegas. So when I went to Salt Lake City the following week I set up lunch with him.

He seemed in better spirits than at the airport. He said Amaryllis was talking to Compusoft about the seismographic system.

"Sell software to Compusoft?" I said. I made the joke about Eskimos and refrigerators. But it was no joke. Apparently Compusoft never cracked the oil exploration market, and they wanted a version of the Amaryllis system tailored to the Compusoft *Overview* system. It would be possible for engineers to use it in the field on their smart phones.

Roger and Maribeth together flew to Seattle to sell the idea to Compusoft. Now Maribeth would head the design team.

Roger didn't have to tell me there was a lot at stake here. Riding on the coattails of a giant like Compusoft could make Amaryllis successful overnight.

But Roger seemed unfocused, more interested in talking about the trip to Seattle than the Compusoft deal. He talked a lot about Maribeth, how well she'd done in the meeting with the Compusoft engineers. "She answered all their questions, kept them on the edge of their chairs," he said, and trailed off.

I told him it all sounded great. Then I took a chance. "Roger," I said, "how's your family?"

He blushed faintly before answering. "Fine," he said, "they're doing fine." Doing fine, it turned out, back in Buffalo. Roger left them there for the kids to finish the school year.

I had this image of Cupid flying around with our twenty-million dollars in his quiver.

* * * *

Back in my office, I called a venture capital guy I knew in California. I made some conversation, asked about a company he was dealing with, and so on. As I hoped, he asked me what I was doing.

"Same old stuff," I said. "Buying and selling companies, arranging financing." I mentioned we were also involved with Amaryllis.

I could almost hear his heart beat faster. "How're they doing?" he wanted to know.

"Don't quote me," I said, "because this isn't supposed to be public, but they're on the verge of hatching up something with Compusoft." No, I told him, our shares weren't for sale. "Do you think I'm crazy?" I said. I said I wasn't able to find any others for sale, either, even though the Compusoft thing wasn't widely known. "I guess they're pretty well locked up until the next offering," I told him.

* * * *

Fact is, Amaryllis *did* sign a contract with Compusoft to produce a prototype system. But it never went beyond that. The Amaryllis *Overview* system died on the vine when Compusoft was unable to get their *Overview* system to fit on a smart phone.

Roger stopped calling me. Became hard to reach. He lasted another six months at Amaryllis, before resigning after "disagreements with management," as *eVenture* put it.

The day Roger left, Amaryllis reported their first period of declining sales. Their venture capital funding quickly dried up, and the company itself was dead before the year was over.

I hear Roger is on the West Coast now, regional sales manager for one of the computerized work station companies, doing well, I'm sure.

Maribeth is at Cal Tech, working in their virtual reality lab, inventing bigger systems.

About the twenty-million bucks we invested: we actually did well, even though the stock eventually plummeted. A few weeks before the Compusoft contract was announced, some hot-shot venture capital guy from Silicon Valley took those shares off our hands. He offered us fifty-five-million before I finally gave in. Evidently this guy heard some rumor about Compusoft's hatching something up with Amaryllis, and he didn't want to miss out. Who could have told him that? I didn't ask.

Condolences

Tonight I'm on foot, till 2 a.m. I grew up in this neighborhood, walked this beat 18 years. I know my way around, know these people. Still, I'm surprised to see Lucille, less than twelve hours after the funeral. People are all over the street, young people, the women in high heels, men in bright shirts. Things are starting to get noisy: a car radio turned up loud, young guys calling across the intersection, the usual Saturday night. But Lucille's got the grandchildren with her, stepping off the curb outside the Handi Mart at the corner of 113th Street.

Me and Lucille are old friends, grew up together, in this neighborhood around Kennedy Square, which isn't a square at all, just the intersection of 114th and Central, one block up from here.

Right now people are everywhere, haven't settled into any particular bar for the night. Somebody's propped the door of The Green Parrot open with a cement block. Inside, a guy tests the microphone with loud talk. A woman laughs.

In the middle of it all, Lucille has a half gallon of milk in one hand, both the grandchildren holding her other hand. This morning she buried her youngest daughter. She's changed into shorts now, but still wears the same necklace she wore this morning. I can't think what to say.

I say to her, "It sure is humid tonight."

Two girls go by, smile at me. One calls out. "Hey, Perkins!" she says. I don't answer, don't pay attention to her.

I know these people, a lot of them since they were kids. Sometimes during the week I'm in the patrol car, covering the whole 18th and 19th wards. I was on Detectives three years, the last eight months of that Undercover. That was it for me. In and out of buildings, busting through doors and windows, never knew who was going to shoot at you, never knew who you might have to shoot, never knew if you were accidentally going to waste some kid — some kid you saw grow up. Never knew if you might *have* to waste some kid. Now this thing with Lucille's daughter: dead when they found her, some house over on King Street. I didn't hear about it until I came on duty that afternoon. All I could think then was, *Thank God it didn't happen on my shift.* As if that made any difference.

This morning at the cemetery, women from the church minded these two grandchildren. There by the grave, right in the middle of the prayers, the women from the church had to keep whispering their names, "Tanicia! Ahmad!" trying to get them to stay put. Every five seconds it was "Tanicia! Ahmad!" trying to get them to be quiet, trying to get them to mind. Still, they were all over the place, dodging around the grey stones.

Lucille didn't seem to notice any of it, there by her daughter's grave, wrung out with crying. This daughter was her baby, just nineteen, already the mother of these two kids: Tanicia, four, Ahmad, two. Now Lucille has buried her daughter, has these two grandchildren to take care of. Tonight she's in shorts and sandals, still wearing that necklace, from church, thin silver flower petals on a chain.

Leaving the cemetery, I took the pastor aside, took two twenties, pressed them on him. I told the pastor it was best they come from him. I couldn't give the money to Lucille myself. I couldn't really face her then, couldn't talk to her. I just didn't know what to say to her.

Now I say to her, "This humidity sure has been something."

Across the street, in front of The Palms, a guy I brought in once acts like he doesn't see me, thinks maybe I don't recognize him. When this guy was 15, 16, we brought him in twenty times before he finally got locked up. Now he must be 18, back on the street.

This morning in the church, someone fastened white ribbons to the pews. Lucille, still a fine looking woman, black dress, high heels. In church she hugged these two close. I want to get away from the funeral, but it's all I can think of. I say to her, "It sure was hot in that church." Her daughter was just nineteen, already mother of these two. They say Lucille got her into nurse's aide class at the community college, started last month.

But her daughter was on the street, sometimes late at night, not always with the right people. I never talked to her. I *thought* about talking to Lucille, then I thought, maybe it would turn out okay. What could I say: "I don't like your daughter's friends"? I didn't know what to say, whether to say anything.

Me and Lucille were kids together; I went to school with her man. We all three covered this territory together, all up and down Central. Sneaking into the subway, stealing fruit from the stands, down at the old Haymarket.

It's not like that today, though. Today, with these kids, it's different. They're on the street, all hours. I see them. Seems like half the homicides I cover are kids, killing each other.

I try to think of something else, but I say to her, "It sure was hot in that church this morning." Lucille nods. She's changed out of her good clothes, still wearing the same necklace she wore in church. A silver necklace, silver flower petals on a chain.

She's quiet now. She has these two little ones. Her daughter named them Tanicia, Ahmad. And Lucille, at her age, starting all over. After watching Lucille's first three, how good they were, nobody imagined anything like this with one of *her* kids. Her boy's in the Navy, just back from the Gulf. Strong kid, like his daddy. Two other daughters, both on their own. But now she has these two grandchildren. She reaches down to straighten the little boy's Giants shirt, and that necklace makes a sound, those silver flower petals tinkling against each other. I don't know what to say, don't know if she's listening.

I say to her, "It sure has been some day." I don't know if she hears me or not. Both these little ones, Tanicia, Ahmad, pulling this way and that. Now here she is, starting over. Her daughter was only nineteen.

Her man: he was a strong kid. Me and him played baseball together at the 115th Street playground. He worked over at the bank, nights, cleaning. He was solid, finished high school, enlisted along with me. That baby was two months old when Lucille got word about her husband. After she lost him, Lucille held on to that baby. Held on for nineteen years.

I tried to imagine if her man had lived. What would he look like? What would he be doing back here? Maybe on the force with me? He would know what to do with these two little ones, his grandchildren, Tanicia, Ahmad, pulling in every direction, one crying for gum, the other wanting a plastic ring for her finger. He would know what to say to Lucille.

I say to her, "It sure is something." Back then they flew me along to escort her man's body back. At the cemetery I was the one saluted, gave Lucille the flag. That time the women from the church had her three older ones to take care of. Her own behaved, of course. She held the baby herself. It slept through the pastor's prayers. I had to walk up to her then, right there by her husband's grave. I had the red beret just right, my boots spit shined. Lucille, nineteen years younger, wearing this same necklace, holding that baby. I said my part, saluted, gave her the flag. It was awkward: she had to put the baby on her shoulder to get a hand free to take the flag, and the baby woke up. I was embarrassed, didn't know what sense it made, waking the baby up for that. After the ceremony, I didn't know what to say to Lucille. When her sister and brother-in-law came up to her, I got on out of there.

Nineteen years later, that baby was on the street, out late, not always with the right people. Was there anything I should have done? Was there anything I *could* have done? Even if I told Lucille, would it have made any difference?

This morning the two older daughters were there, with their own little ones. The son was there in his Navy blues: a strong kid, like his daddy. On leave from the *Saratoga*, just back from the Gulf. And then these two grandchildren, running all over, wouldn't sit still.

I never had kids, but I knew, watching my sister, watching Lucille. You have four, like Lucille. It looks like the first three are doing okay. They get good grades, finish school, get good jobs. Then, somewhere along the line, something happens. The fourth one, she starts spending more time away from home. Maybe you don't like some of the people stopping by for her. But you don't want to believe anything's wrong. People say you've babied her, held her back. You want to give her a chance, but before you know it, you've lost her.

Lucille's first three, they did okay. But her baby, her youngest daughter... Somewhere, something happened, she lost this youngest daughter. She held her back, then she lost her. I saw it happening, but was it my place to tell her? What could I say to her? Would it have made any difference? Now here she is, with these two grandchildren, this same necklace.

If this happened to my niece, to one of my nephews, I wouldn't know what to do. I don't know how I would stand it. I want to tell Lucille I know how she must feel. I want to tell her I wish I had done something. Instead I say to her, "That was a good crowd there this morning, in that church." But I don't know if she hears me. The two little ones are pulling in different directions. One wants to go back in the Handi Mart. I don't know if Lucille hears me, standing there in her shorts and sandals, still wearing that necklace, starting all over with these two little ones.

So I take two quarters, take the littlest by the hand. I put one quarter in, hold the boy's hand under the metal spout, crank until it stops, and six, seven little square chewing gums — red, yellow, green, blue — pop out into the boy's hand, and he stares at me. With the other quarter I show the oldest how to work the crane. I show her how to work the crane, get the ring she wants, and she thanks me, putting the ring on.

The littlest, Ahmad, he just stands there, holding the chewing gums, staring at me. So I take one of the chewing gums, throw it up in the air, catch it with my mouth. Even Lucille smiles at that, tugs the boy's hand. The boy stares at me. Lucille can't get the boy to say thanks, can't get him to say anything. Finally she thanks me herself.

But before I can answer, before I can say anything, before I can even think, she hugs the half gallon of milk closer, gets both the children by the hand again, starts across the street. Finally I think to step out in the intersection, put my hand up to freeze traffic. But they're already on the other side, Lucille helping the boy up the curb. Her granddaughter, Tanicia, stops for a second. She has the ring on, looking at it. She holds it out under the street light, turning her hand this way and that to see the sparkle.

"Condolences" in *Calliope*, Volume 15, Number 1, Fall/Winter 1991, received Special Mention in The Pushcart Prize XVIII, 1993-1994.

The Blessing

Skittering up the embankment 200 yards away, the girl in the red dress carried a large black lunch pail. Her father's dinner, Mister Holmes thought.

For a moment he stopped the rhythmic scraping of his hoe between the rows of vegetables. He watched the girl's younger sister — a yellow dress emerging from the field of goldenrod at the foot of the embankment — follow her up toward the state road. Their mother doesn't know about that, he thought.

Since the war started in 1941, the plant operated three shifts, 12- and 14-hour days for the girls' father, a project manager for the new P-38 fighter. Their mother packed the lunch pail with a share of the family's hot meal every evening at 5:15 and sent it off with the two girls. They were supposed to carry it to their father along the narrow, dusty town road. The town road ran alongside the state road for half a mile, then curved under a stone block underpass supporting the state road's rise into the mountains. The state road was widened to four lanes two years before to carry traffic to and from the sprawling war production plants which covered this end of the valley. The plant where their father worked was on the other side of the state road from their home.

It was 5:18 and there was a steady chorus of roaring engines as cars left the plants. The workers would arrive home and open newspapers spilling over with pictures of German concentration camp horrors just then being discovered in the weeks after the war in Europe had ended. With lined maps and broad sweeping arrows the same papers pictured the allies' advance across the remaining dots of Japanese-occupied islands in the Pacific.

On the road to the plant, the workers were packed three in the front seat and four in the back, advancing at 50 miles an hour across this once sleepy Pennsylvania valley. Some of the drivers were wrinkled men whose age kept them from the war and whose pride brought them to the factories 50 and 60 hours a week. They turned over to their wives the tilling of victory gardens carved into the sides of mountains in hamlets too high and deep within the grey mountains to know the roar of the state road coming out of the valley below. Others were frustrated young draft rejectees. In this five-mile stretch of concrete highway, emerging from the gates of three different plants, each driver had a chance in his own imagination to become a daring pilot roaring down the runway at the controls of one of the fighter-bombers assembled here in the valley. Each day at this time, the concrete roadway became the steel mesh runway of an emergency U. S. air base planted in the sand of an unknown Pacific island eight thousand miles away.

Instead of walking the extra half-mile down the town road to the underpass allowing them to go safely under the roaring state road, the girls climbed the embankment against their mother's orders, as Mister Holmes had seen them do before, to cross the state road. First they would easily cross the two eastbound lanes, nearly empty except for a few scattered late arrivals for the evening shift. They would stop long enough on the two-foot-wide grassy median strip to lean on a telephone pole and catch their breath. And when there was the least break in the line of roaring warriors streaming down the road, they would dart, laughing and screaming, across the two westbound lanes leading from the plants into the mountains.

Mister Holmes saw the red dress with the huge black lunch pail and the smaller yellow dress disappear through an opening in the wooden fence supposed to keep trespassers off the busy state road. He vowed to tell their mother first thing the next morning, knowing he wouldn't. His fear for the girls' safety was tempered by memories of far more reckless exploits he carried out as a child in this same valley, not to mention in the caves and crevices of the surrounding mountains, before the state road was built.

Mister Holmes gazed at the opening in the fence for another second. Then turned his attention back to his garden. The cabbages were finally starting to come around, but only after ten weeks of battling the scrawny brown rabbits foraging through people's gardens, their feeding grounds destroyed by the massive wartime construction that took over the valley three years before. Even on some of the healthy cabbages there were marks of earlier rabbit nibbles now healed and grown over. And the rows were by no means full. The spacing of the green, leafy clusters was frequently broken where whole plants had been chopped off by the wild rabbits: two plants missing here, another there, every other plant at the end of that row, four plants in a row there on the edge.

Mister Holmes bent down and pulled up a weed between two rows, straightened up and threw it aside, out onto the lawn he mowed earlier. Turning back to take his hoe in both hands, his eyes again scanned the embankment along the side of the state road, scanned it a second time, then froze. Mister Holmes put his left hand up to shade his eyes and somehow bring the picture closer.

"My God!" he said out loud. "My God! No!"

Winding up the embankment, his blonde head barely showing above the tall weeds, a small figure worked his way toward the opening in the wooden fence through which the red dress and yellow dress disappeared minutes earlier.

This was the boy John. His sisters were nine and seven, but John had been born since the Barr family moved into the house next door two and a half years ago. He couldn't be two. Probably more like 20 or 22 months old. Though in bed toward the end, Mom Holmes was still alive during the time Mrs. Barr was pregnant with John. Mister Holmes moved his wife's bed closer to the side window where she would smile and wave to the girls playing in the yard.

Mom Holmes stayed alive to see the child born. And the day he was given the name John, the two girls scrambled into her room and up onto her bed, bringing her a gold and white napkin and cake from the baptism party, crumbs of cake and icing and little silver pellets of decorative sugar falling everywhere and sticking in the folds of the dark-hued afghan covering the foot of her bed.

Mister Holmes' favorite memory of recent years was of the boy being carried that day to his wife's bedstead. In contrast to the girls' wild rush, the boy lay peaceful in the white blankets, his eyes closed, not smiling himself, but reflecting off his tiny nose and chin all the radiance of his mother's proud face as she held him down for Mrs. Holmes to touch.

Mom Holmes lived only two weeks longer, but without the pain she suffered for over a year. Her last two weeks were peaceful and serene, and it was a gift to Mister Holmes to be able to remember his wife that way. A gift from the boy, John, he thought. It was as if the blessing the old woman bestowed on the child flowed back to her as well, bringing her the baby's own calm and peace in return.

The Barrs brought all three children to the funeral, and Mister Holmes remembered them there by the graveside. He wondered what they understood of Mom Holmes' death.The older girl, who cried at the casket. The younger girl, who asked if Mom Holmes was taking a nap. Mister Holmes wondered when the boy John would learn of death.

Ever since John was old enough to walk, he stood by Mister Holmes in the garden, picking up weeds the old man threw aside, throwing them again with a determined tiny fist. Mister Holmes had seen this boy's determination get bigger as he got older. And he recognized the same determination in the small yellow head pushing upward toward the wooden fence.

Even as he started to run, Mister Holmes shouted at the boy and let out the shrill whistle he used to call his old dog, and had used to call earlier generations of hounds.

"JOHN! NO, BOY!"

But the child had entered the sound field of the cars on the state road just a few feet on the other side of the wooden fence, and did not hear.

Mister Holmes cursed the burden of his 67 years as he ran toward the embankment. He was already past the boy's house, the last house in the row before the town road turned 90 degrees and ran in the shadow of the state road above it. He left the town road at the bend and started across the last 100 yards of field, flooded with goldenrod, to the embankment of the state road.

His whistle and shout alerted the boy's mother, but he barely heard her scream behind him as she came out on her porch, realized what was happening. Mister Holmes was running across a field of chest-high goldenrod the boy had easily walked through unseen a few minutes before. Along the dusty path, a narrow trench, worn by children's slender feet, caught at his heavy work shoes at every step.

Ahead of him and above him, the boy dawdled for a moment at the top of the embankment. For an instant it looked to Mister Holmes like the boy would turn back. But just then he found the opening in the wooden fence, carefully stepped through to the other side, his yellow hair disappearing from Mister Holmes' sight.

Running through the last 20 yards of goldenrod before the embankment, Mister Holmes pictured the road beyond the fence.

The boy could easily make it across the eastbound lanes, nearly vacant now except for an occasional latecomer speeding in for the evening shift. But Mister Holmes couldn't catch him before he reached the westbound lanes on the other side of the road, now roaring with the steady rush of automobiles leaving the plant.

Mister Holmes imagined the boy walking across the first two lanes and climbing onto the elevated grassy median with a determined step. As the old man emerged from the sea of goldenrod and started up the embankment he listened for the blare of horns and screeching of brakes that would tell him he was too late.

But the roar of cars continued unabated, and at the top of the embankment Mister Holmes bent over and struggled through the opening in the wooden fence. As he straightened up he saw the boy on the median, hidden from the oncoming drivers in the shadow of a telephone pole.

The boy had stopped, not looking ahead or behind or at the cars speeding by, but at the concrete surface of the far lanes. There, for the last several days, a rabbit had been run over repeatedly, and was flattened against the roadway like a lifeless brown cartoon character.

Dizzy and out of breath, Mister Holmes forced his legs across the last few yards to the grassy median. There he grabbed the child with both hands, catching the small body up against his chest, holding on for his own life as well as that of the boy. His legs quivered, his entire body shook with the fear of the last two minutes, with exhaustion, with tears of relief.

Unperturbed, the boy tapped him on the ear for attention, then pointed to his new discovery on the roadway. "Bunny Rabbit, Poppa Holmes," the child said. "Bunny rabbit."

Turnaround Time

The tinkling bell on the front door signaled the evening's first customers: an attractive, middle-aged woman and a heavyset greying man wearing a convention badge on his tweed jacket. As Eugene Chen, owner of Buffalo's oldest Chinese restaurant, looked up to smile at his guests, the man struggled with the door and bumped his wife's head. Eugene Chen extended his hand to help, but too late. They were already through the door. He should have propped open the heavy door, as he often did on summer evenings such as this.

Flustered by his awkward entrance, Harold Doebeler looked around for something familiar. The Chinese guy was standing right there with menus. Doebeler took his wife's elbow protectively, held up two fingers and managed a nervous smile. "Mama-San's birthday," he told the owner.

"Oh, Madame's birthday!" Eugene Chen said. "A happy occasion! We give you a good table."

Anita Doebeler smiled at the attention, followed the owner to one of the center tables. "Harold, this is nice," she said over her shoulder.

Third in line on the way to the table, Doebeler sucked in his gut, noticed the Eastern Hardware Dealers Convention badge on his coat, slid it off and into his pocket.

As soon as Eugene Chen heard the word "birthday" he decided on table eleven. In the center of the restaurant, it was reserved for birthdays, anniversaries, graduations — every special occasion. When large groups arrived, Eugene Chen put them at table eleven. He pulled in surrounding tables to make enough seats. Waitresses rushed to rearrange place settings. But not just large groups: sometimes small parties, too. The radiance of lovers should not be hidden in a quiet dark corner. Eugene Chen placed them at table eleven, and lit a single white candle for them.

Often for the celebrations at table eleven, there was a cake with lighted candles. The ceremonial cakes with white icing were the only Western item served in Eugene Chen's restaurant. Compliments of the house.

The custom started with Eugene Chen's own two daughters. Normally they ate at the little table in the corner of the steamy kitchen where the waitresses and the old Chinese cook pampered them. On birthdays they insisted on getting dressed up and having real birthday cakes. They also insisted on table eleven. Seeing the little daughters' parties in the restaurant, guests started asking ahead for the cakes. Now Eugene Chen regularly ordered an extra one every day. The ceremony was part of his repertoire.

He liked best serving the cake on his own initiative, hearing a birthday or anniversary mentioned. Always the youngest waitress brought the cake to the table. The guests were surprised and delighted.

Frequently people sang, often from other tables. Eugene Chen did not know the custom of public singing, but the first time it happened in his restaurant he saw the guests enjoyed it, so he stood by and smiled. His waitresses stood by and smiled, applauded gently when the song was complete. In turn, the guests of honor sometimes shared the cake with nearby tables, the waitresses passing plates of cake back and forth in a clatter of laughter and excitement. If Eugene Chen's wife was not busy in the kitchen, she stood at the back of the restaurant with her arms folded, smiled at the singing and the celebration.

This night, as soon as his two guests were seated at table eleven, Eugene Chen caught the eye of his oldest waitress. He made a small circle with his two hands. She understood the signal for a birthday cake to be iced and decorated for table eleven. Before the two guests opened their menus, preparation for the surprise party began.

Back in the reception area, Eugene Chen contemplated the couple at table eleven. The man had referred to his wife as "Mama-San." Eugene Chen first heard this expression applied to his own mother, when he was four. He became separated from her in the carpet section of Midland Department store. He sat down on a stack of throw rugs and cried. A security guard scolded him. "You should have stayed with Mama-San!" he said. Eugene Chen didn't know this expression, didn't know the man was talking about his mother.

* * * *

"Honey, this is the real McCoy," Harold Doebeler told his wife. "This is a real Chinese place." He discovered this himself as he tried to find on the small menu a dish he recognized. Each item was printed in Chinese characters with a short English description. The stiff yellow parchment menu was a booklet of six pages and more than a hundred items. The last dessert on the list was number 132.

Once a salesman took Doebeler to a Chinese buffet in Wilkes-Barre: all the rice and chow mein and eggs fu yung you could eat; all the tea you could drink; and all for less than two super cheeseburgers and a shake. Before that, in Korea, well, not in Korea, but when Doebeler's transport ship was ferrying troops between Japan and Korea and Okinawa, talk about food — teriyaki, sushi. Sweets, too: these little Chinese pastries — nuts and apricots, sold them right on the street. There wasn't a Chinese restaurant in Prospect Park, and Doebeler promised his wife a Chinese dinner when they came to Buffalo. This occasion was high on their priority list.

The trip was Anita Doebeler's birthday present. It was her wish. "Harold, to see you actually take some time off. Even if it's just for the convention. You've been saying for years we'll go. It would only be a week."

Each time they had this conversation Doebeler's stomach muscles tightened and his shoulders drew closer to the center of his body. Trouble was, Anita meant well, but she just didn't understand the importance of being at your store. Things didn't run by themselves. They ran because Doebeler personally checked everything, and they always ran right. But when his wife brought up the vacation issue a third and then a fourth time, he resigned himself to losing a week.

The young waitress filled their water glasses. The Chinese owner placed a single white candle in the center of the table. A black man and a college girl were now at one of the tables along the wall. Three middle-aged couples arrived together. Doebeler noticed the men were not wearing ties, wondered if he should take his own tie off.

The candle cast a shadow of the water glass over his menu. Doebeler tried to figure out where appetizers left off and entrees began. There were seven types of shrimp, none fried. Where was eggs fu yung? Where was *rice*, for Christ's sake? By the end of page four, Doebeler forgot the choices. Back to page one.

As the restaurant filled, Eugene Chen used looks and subtle gestures to set off flurries of activity like tiny firecrackers in various parts of the restaurant. Occasionally he moved here or there to light a candle, straighten a flower in its vase, pick up a dropped napkin, point to a recommended item on the menu.

Eugene Chen liked to weave a magnetic field around table eleven. He focused the entire restaurant's energy there. He was cordial to each new arrival, but his attention was on the couple at table eleven. They were the anointed ones. The woman's birthday was to be the evening's ceremonial theme. He sensed the precise moment when his guests needed help with the menu, smiled, stepped toward their table.

* * * *

At home Doebeler watched "Nightly Business Report" on Satellite. He recalled a recent report on a chain of coffee shops in New York City and New Jersey. The small shops had only twelve to fifteen counter seats each. Their sales volume depended on customers coming and going in a hurry so new customers could take their places. The company hired monitors to travel throughout the chain measuring the average time a customer spent at the counter. Turnaround time, they called it. When Doebeler saw the Chinese owner approaching his table, he wondered about turnaround time at the "Szechuan Princess."

"Mama-San needs a little more time to make up her mind," Doebeler said as Eugene Chen approached. "Wouldn't mind a little more of your tea, though." He jiggled the pot toward Eugene Chen.

Eugene Chen seldom had to make noise to get anything done in his restaurant. This night, every waitress and several of the guests heard him clap for tea at table eleven.

In the kitchen one of the older waitresses whispered to Eugene Chen's wife. She came to the small round window, looked out, then quietly stepped into the dining room.

By now Eugene Chen was back in the reception area, drying his hands on a red napkin. He smiled at her. Quietly she smiled back, but remained outside the kitchen door in the rear of the dining room, pretending to fuss over the waitresses going back and forth.

Doebeler finally settled on shrimp, shrimp something-or-other. Number twenty-eight. He read the English description to the young waitress. "And how about some rice on the side," he added.

The young girl started to smile, then touched her pencil to her lower lip. "The Szechuan shrimp is served on rice," she said.

"Well, that's what I meant," said Doebeler. "There's rice *with* it." It wasn't always easy dealing with these people, he thought. He only wanted what was coming to him. But he could see his wife was enjoying the evening. Hell, that's all that counted.

* * * *

By the time dinner was being cleared away at table eleven, Eugene Chen was determined to make the evening's finale a success. The older waitress told him the cake was ready. He waited for the table to be cleared, then with a nod of his head signaled for the cake to be brought in. At the same time he heard the man ask the young waitress about dessert. A *Chinese* dessert, the man said.

Startled to hear the request at the very instant the surprise birthday celebration was to begin, the young waitress turned to Eugene Chen with a question in her eyes.

Christ almighty, thought Doebeler. These people are funny! It looks like I actually need Papa-San's permission to order dessert for my wife on her own birthday.

Eugene Chen dispatched the young waitress to the kitchen with a single Chinese word. He approached the table smiling.

"There will be a cake for Madame's birthday," he said. Doebeler interpreted this as a question. He chuckled, and waggled two fingers to decline. "We didn't come all the way from Prospect Park to Buffalo to have *cake* for Mama-San's birthday," said Doebeler. "I was thinking about a little pastry I once had over there, sort of a triangular shape," he put his thumbs and forefingers together to make a triangle the right size.

The Chinese owner was not paying attention. He smiled at something happening behind Doebeler. Doebeler swung around in his chair to see the young waitress approaching the table with a small birthday cake.

He meant well, thought Doebeler. Just a little communication problem. "Honey, what a nice cake," Doebeler said to the waitress. "That's awful sweet. I told Papa-San we weren't having cake. We're looking for a little Chinese pastry." What the hell did they call them? All he could think of was to make the triangle again.

Anita Doebeler put her hand on her husband's sleeve. "Harold, the cake will be fine. It's a lovely cake," she said softly.

"What's the name of the nuts? Macadamia nuts," said Doebeler. "It's a small triangular pastry with apricots and macadamia nuts... Honey, leave it to me. I'll buy you the cake, too. I just want you to try one of these pastries. If these people do it right, there's nothing better."

"What you are talking about is not Chinese," said Eugene Chen.

"Now wait a minute, I had it over *there*," Doebeler said. "Don't tell me my memory is going bad."

"Oh, you have been to China?" asked Eugene Chen.

Doebeler looked around. The young waitress stood holding the cake. The candles were starting to burn down. "Well, I'm not a far-east expert, my friend. Japanese, Chinese, I won't swear to it. All I know is I was over there." And by God, he *was* over there. Hauled a hundred thousand troops between Japan and Korea and Okinawa. They sold these little pastries from carts right on the street. "Right on the streets of Tokyo," Doebeler said. Again he found himself holding up the triangular frame of his thumbs and forefingers. He wondered if he perhaps tasted the pastry in Honolulu.

When Eugene Chen heard "macadamia nuts" he knew it was not a Chinese pastry. The macadamia nut was unknown in China. On the streets of Tokyo, he thought to himself. On the streets of Tokyo, it was said that Japanese vendors sold to the occupation forces delicacies made from cat meat.

This thought he was able to hold in his chest, and not speak. Still, he knew what happened at table eleven was a disgrace. The words he spoke to his guest were a disgrace. The tone he used was a disgrace. He wished his words were dead. He wished the feelings beneath the words were dead.

Eugene Chen left the dining area, walked through the front door to the sidewalk. The heat evaporated from his cheeks and forehead into the summer evening. He adjusted the canvas awning and picked up a chewing gum wrapper from the sidewalk.

Through the window, he saw his wife move from the rear of the dining room. She took the young waitress's hands, still holding the cake, and guided them to a place in front of the woman at table eleven. The first notes drifted through the front door as table fourteen — the table of three couples — started to sing.

Harris Steps to the Line

Funny thing, for January: it's stuffy out here in the driveway. Harris tries to get a deeper breath. Mostly blue sky, just a wisp of cloud here and there, and blowing. No more snow for now. He tries to find the shovel. Maybe if he stood up he could see where it landed when he fell.

Of course when you fall you forget everything. He had been thinking about Harris Jr. Something he wanted to tell him.

Where he fell wasn't a slick spot, anything like that. More like the driveway moved. Like the deck of a ship coming up to meet you. Anyway, don't stand up yet. Just hold on a minute … Here it goes again.

Harris looks for a fixed star, settles on the white knob at the peak of the garage roof. Tries to focus on that white knob, keeping everything level. Tries to hang in there, holding on with his eyes.

Then it gets quiet, the wind stops. What comes into focus is the backboard and rim mounted at the edge of the garage roof. It's an old picture, fuzzy, no color, like 1950s TV. No wonder: he's lost his glasses. Must have landed the same place as the shovel.

The wind has let up, the bad air blown over. Easier to breathe now. Always, before he shoots, he bounces the ball twice, sights on the rim. Kids love to come and play here, in Harris's driveway, even watch him play. Hell, half the neighborhood sometimes, lining the driveway. Always lots of kids; even some grownups.

Mr. Harris, someone shouts from a distance. *"Mr. Harris?"* right up in his face now. Kids love to come over here, talk with him, shoot a few hoops, play with his kids.

"Mr. Harris, it's going to be okay." Someone lifts his head, slides a pillow behind it.

Just wait a minute, Harris thinks, get your bearings. When he's ready, he'll edge his toes up to the free throw line, bounce the ball once or twice.

It's going to be okay! somebody says. Who said it's okay? Too many people talking, Harris can't keep track. The pillow feels good, but he wants to lift his head, look beyond the crowd, focus on the basket, the back of the rim. Focus is the key, try to keep it in focus. *Visualize the shot.* Harris stressed it with his kids. Visualize the shot. Visualize the arc of the ball. Visualize it settling into the net.

"Mr. Harris, can I pull your sleeve up?" A guy is talking right in his face again. I know that guy, thinks Harris. It's Bill Mullins. Maybe he says it.

"I'm Jeff Junior, Mr. Harris," the guy answers back, "Bill's grandson."

Harris tries to remember if Harris Jr. played with Jeff Mullins. Is Jeff this boy's father? Whatever happened to Bill? Harris can't remember if Bill Mullins is dead or alive. For that matter, Harris can't remember what he wanted to tell Harris Jr., three minutes ago, back when he fell.

Harris looks up at the rim. He remembers the feel of the ball in his hands, the sound of it bouncing on the asphalt. Except the driveway's starting to move again. Keep the rim in focus.

Neighborhood kids play here all the time. If he comes out, he can't resist showing them tricks, passing behind his back, shooting backward over his head.

Harris taught Harris Jr. in this driveway, on this court. You want to get your kids started right. Teach them fundamentals. And all his grandchildren played. Harris Jr.'s three kids, even his daughter. Laura's four kids — two girls and two boys.

Harris Jr., in high school, playing on this very court. No, not *this* court, start over, it must have been the Providence Armory. Son of a gun, the old Providence Armory. Was the Civic Center built then yet?

This kid, young Mullins, in his face again, asking something. Maybe *he* can find the shovel for Harris, and his glasses, see where they fell. Young Mullins wouldn't know about the Providence Armory. That was during Harris Jr.'s time. What did Harris Jr. do in high school? Was this what he wanted to tell him? Final game, the championship, they won it. Harris Jr. played the game of his life, poured in 24 points. Wait a minute! Start over! Maybe that was the semifinal. Because didn't they lose the championship that year?

Harris Jr. loved basketball. Took after Harris. Grandchildren? Hard to keep track. Wasn't Laura's oldest picked for all-state his senior year? Laura played tennis, but her kids got the basketball genes anyway. Now Laura's a grandmother. Talk about unbelievable!

Whoa! Here goes the driveway again. Hold on! Ride it out! Harris can shoot just as good even with everything moving. It's mostly psychological. Visualize the shot. Visualize the arc of the ball. Visualize the ball settling into the net. Got so you could *feel* when it was right. It wasn't anything you saw or heard, you actually felt the ball settle into the net.

When Harris was a kid, basketball was two-handed set shots. When's the last time you ever saw anybody shoot with two hands? One-handed, two-handed, whatever: Harris could adapt his game. That was life, wasn't it? Adapting your game? Every generation had something new you had to learn, just to keep up.

Is Barbara home? somebody asks. Darned if he can remember *who's* home. Ask young Mullins, Jeff Jr., Bill's grandson. He seems to know everything.

Barbara always told him, "Get on out there with your son. Laura and I can take care of these few dishes." That wouldn't pass nowadays. When the grandchildren play at Thanksgiving, they're *all* out there, boys, girls. Girls shooting jump shots, setting picks as good as Shaquille somebody, played for Los Angeles a few years back.

Looks like some of the older kids standing along the driveway now. Some of the neighbors, mothers and fathers, little kids in the front row. They all must be watching Harris, waiting for him to put the ball in the basket. *Did anybody call Laura?* somebody asks. I didn't call *anybody,* Harris thinks.

Resurfaced the driveway once, new asphalt over the old. Moved the basket and rim up an inch and a half to keep it exactly at ten feet. No unfair advantage, he told Harris Jr. It's ten feet at the Providence Armory, you practice at ten feet here in the driveway. Actually that was a while back. What was that neighbor's name? Helped him put the basket up. But a little sloppy with his measurements. Harris came along behind him, measured everything again.

No hard feelings, though. Life is too short for that. The neighbor's kid still played here, day in, day out. The best court in the neighborhood. Regulation distances: free throws, college and NBA three-point shots. If the driveway would just steady up, stop moving. With everything moving like this, measurements don't mean a hell of a lot.

Wouldn't the neighbor love to hear that, coming from Harris? *Measurements don't mean a hell of a lot.* Maybe that's what he should tell Harris Jr. — the thing about measurements. Neighbor's dead, that's for sure. Years now. Him and his wife both. His kid lived in the house a year but the kid's wife wanted something newer, who knows what. Another family bought it from them. Coorsens? Probably even before that. Anyway the neighbor was number 17. Coorsens were the red shingles, number 21. Whatever.

Damned driveway. Harris is getting a little light-headed. Might help if he could find his glasses. Get everything back in focus. The embarrassing thing is: Harris remembers Coorsens, but what in the hell was the neighbor's name? Man lives beside you twenty, twenty-five years, you ought to remember.

All these people standing along the driveway, mothers, fathers, kids: doesn't anyone remember the neighbor's name? Does anyone here live at number 17? Does anyone here remember Harris Jr. in high school?

Is that the only blanket you could find? one of the mothers wants to know. Why did a game always attract people? Everybody loved a game.

Maybe the fire truck attracted the people. No, start over! It's not a fire truck. It's the other thing driving up, the red light and so on. People love the fire truck, the red light, whatever. People love a game. The neighbors. The kids. All here to watch.

Now it's a fireman in Harris's face, a little guy. His badge says Spinos, Spinosa, something like that. Mr. Harris, he says. "Mr. Harris?"

Ask young Mullins, Harris thinks. Jeff Jr., Bill's grandson. He knows everything. I've answered all his questions. What I can't remember is what to tell Harris Jr. Maybe about high school? About one of his games?

Harris is surprised to see Barbara home from work. My God, Barbara, don't leave your purse there on the pavement. *Is it all right if I take his shoes?* she asks. She usually just keeps tabs on things from inside. "Honey, let me take those shoes," she says.

You remember those shoes, Barbara? We got them that day. Was it a Thursday? Friday? I took the day off. We went to lunch. Anyway, they're just regular shoes, right? Slip them right off, Barbara, and I'll step to the line like that, shoot the ball in my sock feet. It's all in the release, anyway. Release the ball at the right moment. Is this where you wanted to be all along, Barbara, out here in the driveway?

People all over, lining the driveway, waiting for him to shoot the ball. The fireman — Spinos, Spinosa? — wants to take his pulse, see if he's up for it. People love a game. Only thing is, if they can't get the driveway leveled out, there's not going to be a game. Maybe that's why Barbara is home early.

The night Harris Jr. poured in 24 points: there were eleven thousand, two hundred in the stands, standing room only. Harris and Barbara just hugged each other and cried when the buzzer went off. That was the semifinals. The next night, in the championship game, Harris Jr. missed the free throw in the last minute. Of all things, to miss a *free throw,* after the thousands he practiced here in the driveway?

Now Harris remembers it. Of all things, to miss a free throw? That's just what he was thinking when Harris Jr. walked off the court after the final buzzer, looked up into the crowd and caught Harris with that expression on his face: Of all things, to miss a free throw?

Now Harris has a lump in his throat, which is no good, doesn't contribute anything. He figures it is time to shoot the ball. Time to focus, right? Harris steps to the line, bounces the ball again, focuses on the rim, the back of the rim, that spot just this side of the back of the rim, where the ball will drop through, settle into the net.

"Let's put this across your chest, Mr. Harris," Spinosa says, fastening a belt, young Mullins helping him. Jeff, or Jeff's son. Whatever.

The driveway crowd starts to rally a bit, starts to lift him up. Harris knows they want it, want to see it, see what they came for, see him nail this shot.

It's darker now. Sun's lower. Hell, it's January, won't stay light forever.

Harris steps to the line again, sock-feet toes on the line. Didn't know Laura would be here. Now he can ask her if it was her kid? Was it your kid, Laura? Was he selected for the all-state team? Did I teach him okay? You want a kid to shoot the ball correctly right from the beginning. Not learn wrong, get in bad habits.

"It's okay, Daddy," she says, not smiling. *Hold his arm,* somebody else says.

Wait a minute, Laura. It's not okay. Start over. Forget about correctly. Forget about bad habits. Forget about measurements, the exact distances. Let them play. Let them have fun.

Actually, *nobody* is smiling. Harris can't believe all the long faces. Hey, lighten up, everybody. It's just a game. Probably could use some clowning around, but not now, no time remaining. Anyway, he can feel it coming now. He feels in control of the ball. This is what he taught Harris Jr. It's a matter of keeping the rim in focus, maintaining control, visualizing the ball going through the rim, settling into the net.

But this is not about going through the rim, Harris thinks. This is about missing.

Of all things, to miss a free throw. Today it would be different, Harris thinks. If Harris Jr. missed the free throw today, it would be different. Harris wouldn't say a thing. At the buzzer he would pick his way down to the floor, get to his son right before he went in the runway to the dressing room. And he wouldn't say anything. Hell, what could you say? He wouldn't say anything, wouldn't even think anything, wouldn't have any expression on his face. He would just put his hand on his son's shoulder, try not to embarrass him.

And this is what he wanted to tell Harris Jr. He wanted to put his hand on Harris Jr.'s shoulder, wanted to tell him it's okay, that it's better than okay, that he's proud of him.

Actually, he can't see him here. Is he here? Maybe not. Maybe it's just these kids, these little ones. Maybe he can tell *them* it's okay. Anyway, he winks at the kids, and they laugh. Seeing this, the grown-ups smile. That's it, he thinks, lighten up.

And he takes a deep breath. Feels the ball against his right hand. Dips his knees. *Somebody hold the door.* Spinosa the fireman, talking over the top of everybody. But Harris keeps his focus, dips his knees, straightens up. Pushes. Pushes with his wrist, his arm, his whole body. At the right moment, lets it go. *Hold the door. Take him right in.*

The ball rises, gains momentum, follows a long, slow trajectory, over the rim and backboard, over the white knob at the peak of the garage roof. Easy now. Okay. It passes over the line of spruce trees beyond the garage, fades into the darkening eastern sky.

Exhausted, Harris lets his arms and legs relax, feels the ball disappear, feels the ball settle into the space beyond. He feels the rush of air, feels the sound swell up within him. Easy now, Harris thinks to himself, the sound rising beyond the reach of his arms. Easy now, he thinks. Okay.

If you enjoyed *It Won't Stay Light Forever*, you won't want to miss Ed Weyhing's novel *Speaking from the Heart*.

Look for more details at www.edweyhing.com.

Excerpt from *Speaking from the Heart*

And then Marvin Kindola was gone — just like that. He didn't say goodbye; he wasn't seen leaving; he didn't check out of his apartment. He just stopped being around.

It sounded as if the Gang may have passed sentence. For sure, Mbasa Kilu didn't want anyone to draw any conclusion about his being involved; or that he *knew* where Marvin Kindola could be found. So he kept his thought to himself, not even sharing it with the brothers.

Instead, in a few days Brother Jerome Jenkins came to him, holding the front section of the Sunday paper. He showed him a headline on the front page, below the fold: *Gang Hit Takes Labor Exec;* and under that: *Gambling Debt Suspected.* Marvin Kindola's body had been uncovered in the brush, fifty meters from the highway between Brightwood Crossing and Oil City. He had been shot twice in the back, then through his ear and out the other side — a gang trademark. The brothers made little or no comment when they heard the news. Mbasa Kilu sensed that none of them were surprised.

* * * *

Two more visits to Ofi Leiya ended with an innocent goodbye kiss from her, after an evening of small talk, without Mbasa Kilu's getting up enough courage to say he loved her — much less that he wanted to be her husband, that he wanted her to be his wife. He treasured her kiss, but was paralyzed at the thought of trying to return it — afraid of making a fool of himself. He made up his mind that on the next visit he would speak up and tell her. Ofi Leiya had invited him for dinner the following weekend — the perfect opportunity. He would tell her what he had never been able to tell her. He would ask her the question he had always been afraid to ask.

What he didn't know was that the next visit would take place three days earlier, on a Wednesday afternoon. He was surprised when Ofi Leiya showed up at the compound. Mbasa Kilu was in his overalls, trying to make himself useful while a guest of the brothers: he had spent the day with Mark Ndiko, trying to help him make sense of Miss Rose's rules for rotating yams in their bins so they all would get air and none would spoil over the winter.

Ofi Leiya had gotten off early from the store and was waiting on the porch of the brothers' house when he returned from the storage barn. She smiled when Mbasa Kilu approached, but the look on her face told him she was concerned — even afraid.

Mbasa Kilu apologized for his appearance and sat down on the porch opposite her. Apparently a message was left on her cell phone overnight. She played the message for him. "We know what you know," said a voice he did not recognize. "*Where did Marvin Kindola have his money?*"

Mbasa Kilu's first tendency was to ask, *What money?* Marvin Kindola had lost heavily when the referee, William Wamp, had double-crossed him. Marvin Kindola would be broke, or nearly broke, unless he had saved an unusual amount — and his lifestyle was not that of a saver.

"What could this be about?" said Mbasa Kilu, half to himself.

"Maybe . . .," said Ofi Leiya, and hesitated.

"Maybe what?" said Mbasa Kilu.

Ofi Leiya took a deep breath. "A month or so ago, Marvin Kindola came to talk to me. He had started an account in the bank. For Martin's education, he said. He wanted to do something to try to make it up to Tedu Ngraeba."

At first Mbasa Kilu wanted to cry fraud: that Marvin Kindola would pretend to do anything to make it up to the man for whose death he was indirectly responsible.

Then it all came together for Mbasa. The Gang was no doubt keeping tabs on Marvin Kindola. They saw him go to the bank, then to see Ofi Leiya. They immediately made a connection, assumed they could find out from her where Marvin Kindola's money was and retrieve some or all of it. And once the Gang got set on such a course, they considered it a point of honor to take it to its conclusion. At the moment, someone in the Gang was convinced that Ofi Leiya was their key to riches, and for this she was in danger.

Mbasa Kilu's mind jumped ahead — to someone more vulnerable even than Ofi Leiya. "Where is Martin?" he asked. It was a day Martin would get off early from Day Care and spend the afternoon with her at the store. "He is at the store. Velma is keeping him until I get back," said Ofi Leiya, "Mr. Munkasy's wife. I'll pick him up on the way home."

"Better you not head home tonight," said Mbasa Kilu. He knew Mark Ndiko would be known at the hardware store, so he caught him before he changed out of his work clothes and asked if he could pick up Martin and bring him back to the compound. "Something has come up," he said. "He should be brought straight back here."

Everything needed attention at once. He went to Brother Jerome Jenkins' office and told him about the mysterious phone call Ofi Leiya had received, that he interpreted it as coming from the Gang. He believed Ofi Leiya was in danger. Brother Jerome Jenkins agreed Ofi Leiya should not stay at her home. Brother Jerome arranged for Ofi Leiya and Martin to stay with Miss Rose in her apartment in the compound until things were straightened out. Miss Rose agreed, reassuring them that she would keep the two of them safe. "It's my apartment," she said, "and it is nobody's business who I have staying there." Mbasa Kilu knew that she had not missed a word of the conversations of the last hour, and thus realized the importance — the danger — of the situation.

For now, at least, everyone agreed that keeping Ofi Leiya and Martin safe was the number one concern.

Ed Weyhing

Ed Weyhing was an avid reader and writer from childhood on. He graduated from the University of Notre Dame and San Diego State University, and served in the U.S. Navy. After that he was a co-founder and president of a computer software company. Retiring young, he was able to follow his enduring interest in writing fiction. He received his MFA in writing from Vermont College of Fine Arts. Many of his published short stories and several new ones are contained in this volume. He is also the author of a novel, *Speaking from the Heart*. Until his death in 2016, he lived in Rhode Island with his wife Mary. They were the parents of three sons.

CPSIA information can be obtained
at www.ICGtesting.com
Printed in the USA
BVOW11s1444070917
494197BV00002B/6/P